I0538030

This light novel is printed using OpenDyslexic, an OpenSource font provided by opendyslexia.org that's made to help with readability. Please support their effort.

Heart of Brass

By Morven Moeller

Dreampunk Press

Heart of Brass

Copyright © 2017 by Morven Moeller

All rights reserved.

For more information go to dreampunkpress.com.

Summary: "When Nessie's father died, he left a fund for his wife and his daughter, both of whom had been ill for years. Nessie receives the first ever mechanical heart transplant known in New Briton. But, despite being given the freedom to roam and explore, with her new heart comes a new issue, someone wants the heart for themselves.

With the first friend she's made is 12 years, Dana -- one of her physicians, Nessie must brave a world she'd long forgotten and face what may be a heartless enemy."

ISBN 13: 978-1-938215-22-3

Categories: LGBT—Fiction, SAGA—Fiction, QUILTBAG—Fiction, Lesbian—Fiction, Gay—Fiction, Steampunk—Fiction, Illness—Fiction, Chronic Illness—Fiction, Leadership—Fiction

Page Count: 138

Word Count: ~23,000

~ *For all those Sapphic and Achillean lovers out there.*

"They aren't real you know. Those stars. They're just projections from that contraption over there." Nessie pointed over at the brass dome in the corner of the room. If you laid quiet enough, you could hear its gears clicking together.

Of course, as of late, the room had never been quiet enough.

The young woman hadn't blinked since she'd walked into the room; she was still looking up at the constellation patterns forming on the shaded ceiling.

She'd introduced herself as Dana, which was strange. Dana sounded more like a first name and no one had ever introduced themselves by their first name to Nessie before. It had always been very formal and overly polite.

Dana followed the pinpointed light beams back to the star contraption. "So, that little thing makes all of this?" She waved a mechanical arm above her head. Where it caught the light, the metallic tones glistened or even glared. Nessie had to squint her eyes to watch.

"It does. My father brought it back for me from one of his last trips abroad." She remembered when he'd told her about it. He'd gone on and on about how she'd finally see the stars. He'd been so excited about it, waving his arms around and nodding so furiously that his tiny wire glasses had flown across the room. Luckily, they hadn't broken.

Dana crossed the room and picked up the star projector.

The star patterns on the ceiling jittered and slid to the wall and floor as she flipped it over to look inside.

Eyebrows raising, Nessie had to admit she was surprised. It wasn't some paperweight; the thing came with some heft. The butler had needed to take a seat on her settee and rest after he'd brought it up. By then, Nessie had spent almost two weeks reading up on stars and constellations and the lore behind them. So, when they screwed the pipe into the wall and opened the steam line, she'd talked herself into something so much more amazing than it turned out to be.

Spreading the fingers of her free hand extremely wide, Dana's mechanical middle finger's casing flipped back, like a pocket watch hinge would, at the uppermost knuckle. Inside, there was a built-in pick. She used it to inspect the inside of the star projector. "This is quite extraordinary. Do you know where he got it from?" She put it back down, gently, as if it weighed nothing.

"No." Nessie repositioned her head on her pillow. Her neck was starting to hurt from watching all the different people who'd been milling around her room. "He went to so many exotic destinations that I can't keep one trip straight from another." She closed her eyes. "It was probably somewhere in the Middle-East though. He would always mention having to clean all of the sand out of it when he'd visit me in here and look at it."

When Dana moved, Nessie could tell, even with her eyes closed; she could hear the pistons in her mechanical legs hiss. Sitting heavily on the edge of the bed, Dana picked up something from the metal tray that had been laid next to Nessie by some man in head-to-toe black earlier that day. "Open your mouth."

Peeking, Nessie could see the mercury thermometer in her metal fingers. She opened her mouth.

The people who'd invaded her home recently kept doing this. They kept checking her temperature and giving her medicine, some of which had names that even Nessie's extensive reading had never come across. They would brew some of it into bitter teas, or they'd grind it into a powder and sprinkle it over her fruit, making the fruit taste wrong.

"How long before the doctor will arrive?" Nessie spoke as soon as the thermometer was removed from under her tongue. "I feel as though it's been forever since his last visit."

Chuckling, Dana placed the instrument back on the metal tray. She then picked up another. "I assure you it hasn't been that long. I'm going to check your nose, eyes, and ears."

Nessie let her.

"Is it true that you've never left this house?"

Rolling her eyes, Nessie closed them again since Dana had retreated. "Not entirely. When I was young, I would play out in the garden while my mother would entertain guests for tea." She remembered the strange fashion they'd worn, huge hats and long skirts. Absently, she wondered if that was still the style. She rarely had visitors in the house, and, when she did, they often had to wear specially cleaned clothes covered in bleached gowns.

Dana wasn't wearing bleached gowns. She was wearing a men's cut tunic and white undershorts. From the reactions the black-robed men had made, it wasn't exactly what people expected from women. They would snicker and cough and turn their heads, like it was indecent to even look in her direction.

If Nessie thought she would get away with wearing only her underclothes, her cotton shorts and camisole, she'd never wear anything else. "I became ill before I began primary school, so I never even went into town." She didn't let herself feel pathetic.

The room became silent for what felt like the first time in months. Well, it was silent except that Nessie could hear the clicking gears of the star projector.

"You must feel lonely."

"No."

Picking up the tray, Dana stood; the pistons in her legs hissed and the bed shifted. "Not at all?"

Since Nessie was laying down, it was hard to shrug, especially with all the pillows that her mother and the housekeeper insisted on keeping on her bed, but she managed. Her shoulders made the beaded tassels click together. "I've had my books."

"Books?" Dana sounded skeptical. She shifted the metal tray in her arms, the medical tools made screeching sounds where they shifted. "You're trying to tell me that books are better company than people?"

Nessie scoffed. "Well, my books never argue with me." She turned her head away from Dana, hoping she'd take the hint.

She left the room, the pistons in her legs taking turns making fluid noises.

Dr. Addler didn't arrive until the day before surgery. Nessie would have preferred if he'd come around earlier than that. "How are you feeling, Lady Ailey?"

"Oh, swell. I haven't been able to move around much more than to use the restroom and bathe, and I've had lots of strange men in my room while I've been in various states of undress." She turned her head on her pillow. "I'm sure I'm as good as I can be."

He nodded, seriously. It almost looked like he had listened to what she said, but, from what Nessie had gathered about Dr. Addler, he didn't actually care.

Perhaps that was why she felt inclined to be rude. She hadn't been rude to anyone in a long time. There was no one to be rude to. And if Dr. Addler wasn't paying attention anyway, why would she try to be polite?

While Nessie preferred the company of books over the company of people, it was very hard to be rude to a book. Trust, she'd tried. For an entire month when she was 14, she'd brainstormed ways to be rude to or angry with books. But worse, she realized that they couldn't forgive her or argue back, so what was the point?

Unlike Dana, Dr. Addler stood when he examined her. He was much shorter than Dana, so it may simply have been due to the height difference. "Everything looks to be in order. For the procedure, you'll have to take an anesthetic. He draped his stethoscope over his shoulders so that the ear horn hung on one side and the metallic pad he'd placed on her chest hung on the other.

Nessie wondered if he lifted the horn to his ear if he'd be able to hear his own heartbeat.

"You won't be able to eat anything after lunch."

Maybe he didn't have one.

"I'll be back later tonight to begin your medications. We'll do the surgery first thing in the morning." He offered a slimy grin. He reached up to tilt his hat before remembering that he wasn't wearing one. It probably hadn't made it in past the mudroom. He coughed and brought his hand back down, wiping it on his vest coat, like the embarrassment was sticking to it.

The tell-tale sound of pistons filtered in from the door to the hallway. Unlike the others, Dana would wait at the door to be asked into the room.

"Come in." Nessie smiled a little. Dana might be better than her books, but she was careful not to get too attached; Dana would leave after the surgery, just like all the other heathens in her home.

Dr. Addler turned. He only came to Dana's shoulders.

Nessie wondered if her mechanical legs were fashioned longer than her originals.

"It's arrived." She was holding a bleached, leather-bound box. It was maybe the size of four of Nessie's adventure books stacked on top of each other, maybe smaller; Nessie tended to read long adventure books.

Turning back, Dr. Addler looked as if he was speaking more from formality than out of friendliness when he asked, "Would you like to see it?"

Not really. Nessie didn't want to see anything having to do with the procedure. She just wanted it to be over with so people would leave, so that she could leave. Swallowing the lump working its way up her throat, she shook her head.

Nodding, Dr. Addler pivoted, took the box, and left the room.

Huffing lightly, Nessie shifted in the bed. She was restless. "See, Dana, people are strange." She'd been on mandated bedrest for over a month, as prescribed by the doctor. She'd always been rather faint, but she hadn't been helpless.

"I don't think Dr. Addler counts as people." Dana came forward and removed a satchel she'd slung over one of her shoulders. She set it on the bed, flap side toward Nessie. "I brought you some more friends." She smiled in jest.

Nessie plucked out the first book. She flipped open the front cover to see the Ailey stamp on the inside. It was from their library. She put it on her chest, finding that she wasn't intent on reading at that moment. Instead, she looked up at the fine linens hanging around her room from the ceiling. From what Nessie had read about circus tents, she was certain that it looked like that; whenever she pictured a circus from one of her storybooks, it looked a lot like her canopy.

Despite that Nessie had a settee, like always Dana sat on the edge of the bed. "Are you feeling well?"

"I told Dr. Addler that I feel fine."

Poking at the spine of the book laying forgotten on Nessie's chest, Dana clucked her tongue twice.

Lolling her head around on her pillow, Nessie's neck ended up at an odd angle, but she could look Dana in the eye. "Does it hurt?"

"What do you mean?"

"Does it," Nessie gestured to all of Dana's mechanical limbs, "hurt?"

As if she'd forgotten that she was half automaton, Dana looked down over herself.

Where she was sitting, her white, cotton shorts had ridden up her thighs so that Nessie could see where her tan, freckled skin met metal. There were large staple-like sutures attaching her legs. Just below a ribbon of brass, there was a cylindrical, thigh-shaped vat of reddish fluid. It was probably the fluid that made the pistons function. From the vat, different tubes carried the red fluid to different places in the rest of the mechanics. Some of the tubes fit perfectly into little round holes; others wedged in between the metal plates. They looked similar to the suits of armor that stood in the Ailey's entryway.

Nessie reached down and traced a finger down the closest of the tubes jutting out from the machine.

"It hurt for a little while, but that was because I didn't have the money to keep buying the medication." Dana clasped her hands in her lap.

Her arms had all the same pieces as her legs. They had the same vats and tubes and metal plating. The only notable differences to Nessie were their size and the color of the liquid. Her arms had a more yellow liquid than the red in her legs.

It was because the liquid was a different density. Nessie knew because her father was a bit of a fanatic over automatons. He'd made his living making and selling steam-powered wagons; he'd made beautiful automated vehicles. These vehicles had everything that anyone could want. He'd designed them with lights and dials and gauges and cup-holders; he'd even figured out how to make heated seats.

At the memory of it, she smiled a little. Her father had sulked for over a week when he'd realized that he'd made them too intricate and expensive to sell. Some of his business associates had laughed at him. His investors were angry since he couldn't pay them back if he wasn't selling anything.

Luckily, he'd had the bright idea to create a lower-end model that anyone could buy if it could be mass-produced. Overnight, they'd been rich. He'd moved his process to a factory on the river, just outside of town. He hired half the young men in town to make his vehicles and they'd moved out to the countryside so that Nessie's and her mother's health could be treated.

When Nessie wasn't confined to bedrest, she would tinker in the workshop.

Since her father had died two months ago, she hadn't been down there.

It had all been a whirlwind, ending up where they were now. "So, when my father left the money, he also knew that I'd need medications after the procedure?"

Dana nodded. "It would seem he thought of everything. The itemized budget accounts for it all." She straightened up, popping her shoulders before swinging her arms back, hands landing between Nessie's legs over the blanket.

Fighting the urge to move her legs, Nessie flicked her eyes up at the canopy again, trying to ignore Dana's closeness. But, she still peeked down.

Leaning back on her arms, Dana looked up too. Her shirt draped over her breasts in a way that Nessie had never seen before. It was probably just the way a men's shirt was cut, or maybe it was because Dana had bigger breasts than any of Nessie's other guests had. And that had been maybe two women over twelve years.

Nessie felt embarrassed; her bosom was much smaller in comparison. They weren't even large enough to impede her sight of the doors across from the foot of her bed. Her face got hot and she lifted the book on her chest upright, pretending to read the embossed title on its cover.

Over the book's top edge came a wet cloth.

Flinching, Nessie dropped the book again. Her eyes widened and she tried to look at the cloth despite that it had been laid on her forehead. It was making her cross-eyed.

"You're a little red. You sure you're feeling alright? If you have a fever, we either need to remedy it or postpone the procedure. You can't go into something like this with an infection." Dana laid her mechanic hand, knuckle-side to the cloth, pressing it down.

"I said I'm fine." Nessie bit out, more from embarrassed shock than anger.

Pulling back, Dana raised her hands in a sign of surrender. "Okay, okay." She let her hands drop back to her lap.

Nessie felt like Dana was the only human she'd spoken to in years. And in a strange way, that was true. She hadn't had any visitors since her mother had fallen so ill that she couldn't entertain. There was no one to go collect them. The kitchen staff and butler were the only other people in the house, but they had lives; they'd go into town and they'd go home at night. When they were at the Ailey estate, they often stayed hidden or with her mother.

With her strange style of dress and her brown hair always up in a knot, Dana had been the first person Nessie had really spoken to. Sure, there were the men in the black-robes with a shiny line of buttons holding them closed from their knees to their chin, but they didn't speak to her; they didn't even say please or thank you.

There was Dr. Addler too, but even Dana said he didn't count.

Dana stood, cocking her head to the side and making the tendrils of hair that had made it loose from her bun wisp to the side. "What would you like for your last meal?"

Groaning, Nessie squeezed her eyes closed. "Don't say it like that. It makes it sound like I'm dying."

"Then what do you want me to say?"

"Just ask me what I want to eat."

"Okay, then." Dana clapped her hands together and let them land in her lap, clasped. The metals ground together, but nothing like how the medical instruments sounded when they were on the metal tray. No, this sounded more like a suit of armor, like Dana was Nessie's personal knight in shining armor.

As if.

Dana gave a little smile. "What would you like to eat?"

It was a restless night just like the rest of the last month had been for Nessie. Bedrest was truly horrible. "I'm probably going to have gained twenty pounds when I finally get out of this bed."

As one of Dr. Addler's assistants – the second-in-command for the Ailey Case – Dana was supervising the men in black as they brought in a metal table and set up the room for the operation. "You'll have gained at least that much," she said to Nessie before berating one of the masked-men, "Have you forgotten our procedural method? Bring in all the tables before you started setting up the lights."

"How many of them are there? They all look the same." Nessie tried her best to ignore the fact that she was getting fat. Ignore the fact that they were getting ready to have surgery. Her stomach growled. Ignore the fact that she was hungry.

Taking the lamp from the man and sending him back out of the room, Dana glowered at the door. She didn't turn when she spoke. "I think there are nine nurses on your case." She followed the movements of the next nurse with narrowed eyes.

They each had a different mask, so Dana could probably tell them apart. Some of their masks had circular, goggle-like eye pieces and others had thinner, slanted ones. One had a long beak-like protrusion from the nose and mouth; another had a cylindrical, pig-like snout. Some had tubes attached and others didn't.

Nessie closed her eyes and turned off her brain. There was no use being worried; worry didn't do anything.

Except that Nessie had little else to do but worry. She tried thinking of her favorite places, not real places like her reading chair in her library or the seat at the table that caught the afternoon sun when they had tea. Instead, she tried to transplant – not the term she wanted to use at that moment; she was trying not to think about surgery – remember; she tried to remember places like Howl's Moving Castle and a planet called Exeldus, places from her favorite storybooks.

She'd never traveled, but she wanted to. Before she died, she really wanted to go somewhere exotic.

That's why she was taking a mini vacation in her head; in the case that she didn't wake up from the procedure.

So, she was doing a terrible job of not thinking about it. It was like having an itch she couldn't scratch; in her lifetime of various illnesses, Nessie had suffered more than her fair share of those.

Nessie spent the afternoon exploring the desert plateaus on Exeldus and traveling through the magic portal in Howl's castle. When she opened her eyes, there was a full surgical setup next to her and Dana was sitting on the edge of her bed again. "What time is it?"

"It's almost 10 am." Dana reached over and put a metal hand on Nessie's thigh. "Are you ready?"

Rolling her eyes, Nessie tried to bite her tongue and let her frustration pass before speaking. She obviously didn't wait long enough. "Ready as I will be. Just get on with it."

Shrugging, Dana looked at her face for a long moment. "You're very beautiful."

What? Nessie blinked in response. She tried to remember the last time someone had called her beautiful. It was years ago when her mother bought her a new blue dress to greet her father in. It was back when her mother could still leave the estate. Her father had come in through the mudroom door after a cleanse and change of clothes, taken her hands in his, and told her how beautiful she looked in her new dress.

That was years ago.

Since then, she'd gotten pasty white. She hadn't been in unfiltered sunlight in years. She took a Vitamin D supplement to make up for it, but her skin was paper white heading toward translucent.

Nessie shook her head, her mouth still hanging open from the shock of the sudden compliment. She forced a scoff from her throat, trying to cover the full extent of her reaction. "You must be duly mistaken." She blinked her eyes again, looking away from Dana's open expression. "I am sickly and pale. I would be more likely mistaken for a servant than a suitor."

Put out, Dana dragged her hand back to her lap, skimming over Nessie's gown-covered thigh in the process. It left a trail of cold-hot tingling in its wake.

"We'll be taking very good care of you. The procedure will be long, but you won't notice." She stood up with a lurch.

Walking around the bed, she picked up a face mask with two canisters attached. "It's time." She held it out for Nessie to take.

Slowly, Nessie inspected the mask. It was made of the same bleached white leather that had covered the box that came other day. The tins attached to the respirator had brand new sticker labels on them declaring them anesthetic. She took a deep breath. "So, I just put it on and go to sleep for a while?"

Dana only nodded. It was curt; it made a tendril of hair fall from her bun.

Putting on the mask was easier said than done, especially lying down. The edges of the respirator had to be flush against the skin of her face and her hair kept getting in the way. After a third failed attempt, Nessie spit her hair out of her mouth and glared at the contraption. "Well, I guess you're just going to be difficult.

"Allow me." Dana put a knee on the bed, leaning over Nessie. She reached up and swiped her cold, metal fingers over her forehead, trailing them toward her temples then behind her ears, capturing the straying red hairs. The assistant visibly shivered.

"Are you okay?" It was barely above a whisper.

"Just static from your hair."

Nessie nodded, just looking up at Dana. The assistant couldn't be too much older than Nessie. There were faint lines on her face, but they weren't unattractive. In fact, they drew the eye to her best features, all of them. Her piercing eyes, her sharp nose, her high cheek bones, her dark freckles, her plush lips, her-

"You need to put the mask on."

"Oh, right." Nessie lifted the forgotten mask to her face, pressing it over her mouth until the leather edges were flush to her flesh and securing it in place with its buckle fastenings.

Once it was on, Dana pulled away, sinking until she had kneeled back, settling her bum on the foot she had on the bed.

"How long will it take?" Nessie's voice was muffled by the device.

Dana took a big breath, letting it out through her nose. "Not long." She flicked her eyes over to the surgical setup. "How about you keep talking to me? What's your favorite book?" Her eyes were soft when her gaze returned to Nessie's.

It didn't even take Nessie a second to know her answer. "I love Red Planet. It's about airship pirates. They..." Her brain grew foggy. "They can't land on the planet with the ships, so they, uh, they..." She took another breath. "They have to live off only what they have with them or what they can scrounge up."

"Sounds unrealistic. How would they get food?" Dana was foggy, too. Her face, her voice.

"They have sheep with them. They have huge airships." Nessie's eyes were heavy, so she closed them. "It's like an archi- an arch- it's like islands."

Dana sounded far away. "Oh, okay. And how does it end?"

Body going lax, Nessie wasn't sure if she answered aloud or not. "They all died."

When Nessie awoke, everything seemed off.

It was dark outside the window, but she wasn't sure if it was the first night after the surgery or a fortnight. Part of her even entertained that it was a night earlier than the surgery, that she'd taken an afternoon nap and dreamt it all, that Dana was nothing more than a figment of her imagination.

A loud noise came from the hall, crashing.

It sounded like armor falling.

Startled, Nessie went to get up, but she couldn't. She was pinned to the bed. She tried again with more effort but with no luck. It was as if she had a stack of books on her chest, holding her down with their tremendous weight.

Had they strapped her down? She ducked her head, bending her neck at an odd angle to look down. She was covered only by her white dressing gown, big splotches of deep red on the front.

Blood.

She wanted to scream. Had something one wrong? Was she paralyzed? Was the rest of her body dead weight? She jerked one of her feet and her knee jumped from the bed. Not paralyzed.

Was she having trouble breathing? Her right hand flew up to her chest. The cotton of her gown had grown stiff where the blood had dried and she could feel the wad of gauze beneath. It was padded by the medical wrapping, but it felt... off.

Another crash sounded from the hallway. This time, it was closer than the last.

Hauling in a big breath, Nessie tried to sit up again. She wasn't paralyzed since her legs and arms, well arm – she wiggled the fingers on her left hand to make sure they also still worked – yes, okay, both arms could move.

Grunting, Nessie used whatever stomach muscles she'd managed to retain after a month of bedrest and brought herself to a sitting position.

The room spun and she almost fell forward under her own weight.

Maybe she was still anesthetized.

With more force than was usually necessary, she swung her feet off the edge of the bed.

Another crash sounded, closer again than the last, followed by a yelp.

Nessie's pulse quickened. She felt it in her neck and heard it in her ears. She dragged herself up from the bed, grabbing onto one of the canopy's four posters to stay upright. Holding on tight with her right hand, she wrapped her left arm haphazardly around the base of the post. It seemed to be lagging; it must still been asleep.

Gulping in air, Nessie stared at the door. Whatever was coming couldn't be far, but she was in no position to fight. She was still recovering.

She glanced around the room. Her blood a deafening roar that made it impossible to think straight. Her eyes landed on the discarded ventilator with the anesthetic tins.

Afraid that leaning over would cause her to fall, Nessie squatted and reached across the bed to grab it.

Then there was a gun shot.

Startled, she lost her footing where she hunkered down next to the bed, landing heavily on her knees, causing the wood to crack. She settled there, knowing she couldn't get up and run, pulling the respirator to her chest with her right hand and staring at the door.

It wasn't but a moment before the door burst open.

Dana landed unceremoniously on the foot board of the bed. There would definitely be some bruises. Nessie wouldn't be surprised if there were some cracked bones.

She didn't stay down long. The assistant recovered, groaning. Her hair had fallen entirely from her bun. She looked like a lion, snarling at the intruder, her hair fanned out into a thick mane. She looked feral.

The next thing through the door was a humanoid drone. Other than its torso, it looked very similar to Dana, same legs, same arms.

"You've gotten far enough into this house." Dana kicked the drone in one of the vats of red liquid in its leg. It cracked, spewing red fluid for a moment, before shattering completely. The red liquid got everywhere. It washed over the hardwood floor boards. They'd have to buy a red stain to redo the floors.

The automaton was missing pieces to his outer shell. Dana must've knocked them off earlier. Its inner workings were visible, vulnerable. Gears clicked together in its chest cavity, where they'd usually be hidden by a chest plate. Oil dripped from its shoulder.

Dana kicked at the same leg again, taking the leg off with the force of it. "It's not polite to come inside when you weren't invited." She swung a punch across the drone's metal face.

Its face-plate flew off and across the room, clattering against the far tinted windows.

When Dana attempted another punch, the automaton caught her by the wrist. At the small victory, the exposed cogs in its head whirred even faster.

But it couldn't move. One of its legs was gone, completely useless, since Dana had knocked it across the room.

Where she was still crouched next to the bed, Nessie tried to think of how to help; all she had was a useless body and an anesthetic respirator. She had to think fast, but her brain defaulted into panic mode, afraid for Dana.

The automaton threw Dana across the room by her wrist; she landed head-first on the settee.

Dana looked up almost immediately, blowing hair out of her face and wiping at her now bleeding nose; she must've cracked it on the wooden frame of the couch.

Nessie could see where blood had dripped and was staining the yellow paisley upholstery.

Anger bubbled up from Nessie's gut; Dana was hurt. So hurt that she was staining things with her blood.

An adrenaline rush came with the anger, and Nessie pulled one of the tins from the respirator, lunged toward the automaton, and shoved it, two-fisted, into its chest cavity. The gears popped and grinded, coming to a sudden, screeching halt.

Time seemed to slow down.

The automaton fell backwards, away from Nessie, into the open doorway, following the momentum of Nessie's shove into its chest mechanism. Then Nessie fell back too. She was still crouched near the ground, so she didn't fall far.

The rushing sound in her ears stopped. Her breathing got shallow. It was like she was falling, except she wasn't just falling backward but into herself. It was like she was pulling away from the outer shell of her body, crumpling inward.

She felt woozy and numb.

Metal hands carefully picked her up from the floor and put her up on the bed.

The colors of her canopy and the star projections swirled around like a child's pinwheel.

Her brain wasn't doing much, but she felt a tug at her left wrist then a tug at the neck of her gown then a terribly hard tug in the center of her chest.

It took a second before the world started to come back into focus.

"Nessie!" Dana was still with her, kneeling on the bed next to where she lay. "Nessie!" The trickle of blood at her nose was beginning to dry and her hair deflated from its electrified mane into a mess of frizz.

With her right hand, Nessie reached up and wiped at the blood on Dana's face. "I'm here."

Dana stopped calling her name and just looked over her face before hunching over and pressing her head to Nessie's stomach. "Don't you ever do that again, you hear me?"

"Do what?" Nessie felt like she needed a nap, a very long nap. "What even happened?"

Before Dana could answer, a rapid spluttering sound caught their attention. The automaton twitched and writhed on the floor, its gears spinning and its belts whirring.

It was the first time Nessie ever felt like it was a problem that she could see the door from her bed.

Dana sat back and brought a knee up, her devastated posture replaced by a predator's stance, ready to strike. She pulled her face into a sneer as she watched the drone where is whizzed and lurched and whirred.

Then it settled back down.

Nessie let out a breath she hadn't realized had been caught in her chest.

Then with a burst of cogs and gears, a spider-like device burst from the automaton's head cavity. Eight skinny legs with three joints each, pulsed, like it was doing a push-up, then a spark lit up its body and it scuttled away down the hallway and back down the stairs.

"What the hell was that?!" Nessie couldn't help but yell. That was definitely something that would go on the list of things she wished she'd never seen. It would haunt her nightmares for years to come.

Dana didn't let her guard down. She still watched the door with narrowed eyes and held her hand in a tight fist at her side. "I don't know." She stood on the bed, her shifting weight causing the four posts to move. "Whatever it was, I never want to see one again." She walked to the foot of the bed, looking down at what was left of the automaton. She jumped down, landing on it.

From the sound of it, she managed to crush the bit she landed on.

"I'm going to dismantle this, maybe salvage some parts; he seems to have a similar make to my limbs." Dana took a deep breath then crouched down. When she stood and turned, she was holding a mostly demolished anesthetic tin. "Good thing this didn't have any more anesthetic in it; we wouldn't have seen that spider-thing."

"I could've gone my whole life without seeing that spider-thing." Nessie answered truthfully. She never wanted to think of it again -- ever.

Dana laughed. "Get some sleep, Lady Ailey. I'm sure that tired you out just as much, if not more so, than it did me." She offered a little smile.

Despite her eyes closing under the immense weight of exhaustion, Nessie didn't actually want to sleep. She was still freaked out. "How will I sleep knowing there are evil, creepy-crawly automatons in the world?" She shuddered, fisting the blanket in both of her hands.

Words drifted up from the foot of the bed "I'll look after you. I will guard you from the creepy-crawlies."

And Nessie fell asleep.

The next time she awoke, the world seemed to be in better shape. She didn't feel like she was a puppet with cut strings anymore, although she still had a lot of trouble moving or sitting up.

After sleep ebbed completely away, Nessie realized that she couldn't see or hear Dana, and that frightened her. What if one of the spider thingies had gotten her? "Dana?"

"I'm just here, my lady." Dana's voice came from the foot of the bed, but Nessie couldn't see her.

Nessie relaxed back into her pillow. "Hello." She tried to brush off the embarrassment from freaking out. She was a full-grown woman who'd never had any people in her life; she should not be afraid of being alone.

Of course, until then, her house had always been an impenetrable fortress; impenetrable to bugs, impenetrable to sickness. Nothing bad had ever gotten in before. She'd never felt like she was somewhere unsafe.

Swallowing hard, Nessie closed her eyes, attempting to regain her cool. "So, what are you doing at the foot of my bed?"

"I was attempting to rest after taking the fighter drone apart."

With a whole lot of effort, Nessie managed to sit up. She pulled her legs in, cross-legged, and propped herself up on locked elbows over them.

At the door to her room, the automaton had been disassembled and sorted into piles of pieces. One pile looked to be bent pieces and cracked or chipped gears, obviously unsalvageable. There were other stacks, but Nessie couldn't tell what was so special about them or upon what criteria Dana had sorted.

Amidst the piles, Dana lay on the floor, perpendicular to the bed, like how a hunting dog would lay in front of a fireplace. She was still tight; her shoulders were drawn up into a permanent shrug and her manicured eyebrows were furrowed at the top of her elegant, but bruised, nose.

"Why are you laying down there?"

"I'm protecting you."

"I get that." Nessie flopped backward onto the bed, almost immediately regretting it from the way her chest felt. "Oof." She brought her right hand up to her chest and laid it on top of the medical wrap. "So, how long before the gauze can come off?"

There was shuffling and scratching from the foot of the bed, and Dana stood up from the floor. "It won't come off permanently for a few more days, but it should probably be changed." She rounded the bed and opened one of the side drawers.

Nessie almost protested. When had they decided to put things in her drawers? Did they discover the erotic books she kept in the far back of the other one? She tried not to flush at the embarrassing thought.

Especially if Dr. Addler had been the one to pull them out.

She could imagine him pulling it out, seeing the worn binding, letting it fall open to one of the usual pages, and humming a little. It was a very disgusting image in her head. He was humming and beginning to move his hips in weird gyrations and patterns while looking over the words.

Ew.

"Are you feeling okay?" Dana's concerned brown eyes searched over her face. "You look a little red."

"I'm good."

"Are you sure?"

Nessie dragged her hands up the bed, intent on sulking like an overgrown toddler. "Yes, I'm sure." When her arms crossed, she felt something strange on one of her wrists. Looking down, she noticed what looked a bit like a watch on her left wrist. "What's this?" She let her arms fall apart so she could further examine it.

From the drawer, Dana brought out new gauze, bandages, and safety pins. "If you hold on a hot second, I'll explain everything."

"Everything?" Nessie flicked her gaze over to Dana. "There's an 'everything' amount of things to tell me?"

Dana's stern expression cracked into a smile. "You're adorable."

"I am not; I'm feisty," Nessie argued.

Scoffing, Dana replied with a low, "That you are." Setting the medical supplies on the bed, Dana reached over and began to undo the buttons on the front of Nessie's dressing gown.

Nessie watched, frozen with an epiphany. Dana has seen her breasts, her woefully unimpressive breasts. Nessie's head dropped back and she stared at the ceiling.

"So, I'm going to remove the old bandages and gauze." Dana spread open the front of Nessie's gown and unclipped the safety pins holding the bandages in place. The wrappings had spots of blood just like Nessie's gown and gauze. "Alright. Now, let me get something to clean it."

The surgery tables had come with matching cabinets and had yet to leave Nessie's room, much to Nessie's disdain. She peeked over at the other woman, where she had turned and opened one of the metal cabinet doors. There was a long rip in the back of her tunic shirt, so Nessie could see the plane of her back. She could see where her muscles moved and where her freckles shifted over those rolling plains.

While Dana collected the necessary supplies, Nessie looked down at her chest.

It wasn't what she was expecting.

And she was stuck in a spot between embarrassment, horror, and fear. Her pulse quickened again and her eyes refused to blink as she stared at it.

Between her breasts, at the center of her chest, there was no skin. Instead, there was a diamond-shaped brass plate visible and, in the center of it, was a little hole. She had a hole in her chest. What if germs got in? Why did they leave a hole in her chest?

Was that common?

Questions floated between her ears, but none of them made it out of her mouth. Her mouth had gone dry and seemed to have disconnected from the rest of her body, no longer listening to its orders.

The pistons on Dana's legs hissed when she stood and turned back with the cleaning solution, a cloth, and some swabs. "Okay. So, I'm going to talk you through all of this as I do it. Eventually, it'll be your responsibility to do this all on your own." She uncapped the bottle of saline solution. "But fear not, I won't let you do it on your own until I know full well you won't be messing it up."

Nodding was all Nessie could hope to achieve given her current shock. She managed a miniscule incline of the head.

"Okay, so first you use a cloth to wipe where the skin meets the metal." Dana put the cloth over the bottle's mouth and tipped it, letting it soak into the cloth. After, she righted the bottle and placed it on the nightstand. Gently, she wiped at the edges of the metal, taking away some yellow, crusty stuff that had formed in one spot and some dried blood in another. "Eventually, this will become minimal. I still clean mine, but there's no more weeping tissue or scabs."

Nessie nodded again. Her eyes were trained on Dana's hands, moving with practiced ease.

"Then you clean out the key hole." Moving along, Dana picked up a swab and dipped it into the solution.

"K-key hole?" Nessie stuttered.

"Yep."

"Yeah, okay." Nessie's eyes remained on the hole in her chest.

Dana carefully put the solution-soaked swab into the key-hole and began to clean it. "This takes a bit longer. This will fill with lots of stuff, sweat, dead skin, maybe blood." She pulled the swab out to punctuate her point. "See, pus."

Nessie didn't need to see it; she could smell it. It was disgusting. She gagged and held her breath to stop the next.

"This won't be as bad after a while, either. In the summer, you'll have to give it more time than in the winter since you'll sweat more and when you're upright it has less chance of filling quite like this." Dana disposed of the soiled swabs and threw the cloth into a pile of surgery garments on the metal table.

It was a lot of information and most of it scared Nessie.

Turning back, Dana reached over her to take her left hand and wrist. "This," she motioned to the watch-like accessory on Nessie's wrist, "is your fluid monitor." She pressed the little button on the side so that the reflective cover sprung open, revealing what would usually be a watch face. This, however, revealed that the inside was split down the middle into two halves. The first half had two smaller dials set into the accessory's bevel and the other side was hollow, a little compartment. And, inside that compartment was a brass turnkey.

Pointing to the first gauge, Dana explained, "This one shows your pulse speed. This one," she moved her pointer finger to tap lightly on the next one, "measures blood flow.

And this," she picked up the turnkey, "is the key to your new heart."

Oh, wow.

It really happened. They replaced her heart with a wind-up.

Nessie's head fell back against the pillow. She still couldn't free the questions that were pinging in her head. What happened if she lost the key? Would she have to go to a locksmith? Would the locksmith know what to do? Would she have to show the locksmith her bosom? How did the gauges on her wrist work? Could she take the gauges off or were they permanent?

"I'm going to wind up your heart okay?" Dana slid the key into the hole and watched Nessie's face when she gave the first twist.

It hurt. It was like someone was turning a crank from inside her chest, like they were plucking on her vocal chords or pulling on a fishhook stuck in her ribs.

Either ignoring Nessie's wince or not noticing it, Dana gave it four more turns before pulling the key out. "Since we cleaned out the hole first, the key is still clean." She put it back in the watch-contraption's compartment.

Nessie swallowed.

Taking her usual seat on the edge of Nessie's bed, Dana petted at Nessie's hair, smoothing the straight red locks over the pillows. Sometimes, she'd mix it up, twirling some of the strands around her mechanical finger before combing it back out.

Dana swallowed, as if this was hard for her. "Do you have any questions?"

And with that, the gates flew open and all of Nessie's questions came out, rapid-fire. Luckily, Dana could keep up.

"Why did you leave a hole in my chest?"

"Because you have a wind-up heart."

"Why would my heart be wind-up?"

"Because, there aren't any other body-safe and practical energy sources for it, yet."

"What if germs get in the hole?"

"That's why you're going to clean it at least twice daily."

"What happens if I lose the key?"

"Don't lose the key."

"Would I have to go to a locksmith?"

The question must've caught Dana off-guard because she didn't have an answer for it.

Nessie kept going, though. "Would the locksmith know what to do? Would I have to show the locksmith my breasts? How do the gauges on my wrist work? Can I take the gauges off or are they permanent? Is all of this normal? Do a lot of people have holes in their chests?"

"Hold up, hold up." Dana held up her hands, signaling for Nessie to slow down.

By then, Nessie was breathing heavy and trying to catch her breath, so she obliged without much argument.

Dana's hand returned to her red hair, smoothing it and playing with it. It calmed Nessie much like how Mother used to calm her when she was a child, by rubbing circles on her back. Dana's mechanical fingers felt very human. "The gauges don't come off. They're connected to the arteries in your wrist. Those wounds, however, have already healed and the tubes are made of rubber, leather, and fish skin so the body doesn't seem to treat them the same as it does larger, metal insertions."

"Okay." Nessie nodded. She looked around the room, searching for an anchor, but came up short. Nothing seemed familiar anymore. A surgery was still set up. Her floor was stained an unnatural red. Her door was cracked and splintered. Her books had been removed. Her drawer had been rifled through. "Okay." Her eyes landed on Dana, the new constant in her room. She stared into her eyes and tried to calm herself the rest of the way. "Okay," this last was barely a whisper.

The hand in Nessie's hair came to a fluid stop, instead just lying there, offering her moral support.

Breathing at a normal pace, Nessie licked her dry lips. "So, when can I go outside?"

A small smile graced Dana's face. "Whenever you want."

Nessie's eyes darted to the window. It was still dark outside and she was tired again from all the thinking her brain had managed to cram into the short time she'd been awake. Plus, worrying used up extra energy, which was basically all Nessie had done.

Leaning forward, Dana pressed a kiss to Nessie's hairline, near where her hand was lying. "But not now. Now, you still need to rest. You've got the rest of your life to explore out there."

Nessie got a funny feeling. Looking at Dana, her newest friend, her newest constant, Nessie found that for the first time she didn't have the burning desire to explore out

there. She wanted to explore what they had, just the two
of them.

It was like a perpetual sleepover.

Or at least, that's what Nessie figured it was like. It wasn't as if she'd had a lot of sleepovers when she was growing up.

"I'm glad it was a success," said Mother over breakfast one morning.

Mother, the esteemed Lady Katherine Ailey, was sicker than Nessie had been. Her illness had been brought on by an accident with aether in one of her husband's labs. The unfiltered aether had deteriorated her cells and made her highly susceptible to everything. That was one of the reasons that natural aether was not used to power any mechanisms affixed to a living body.

One of the servants strode up to her mother's wheel chair and offered her a blanket. The older woman passed, her hand waving them away.

While Nessie had never felt alienated from her mother, this was the first time in a long while that they had spoken to each other about something of substance. After years living day-in and day-out in the same few walls, people tended to run out of things to talk about.

Plus, Nessie's mother wasn't much into reading adventure books or tinkering with whimsical inventions. She was much better suited for playing the violin or reading poetry.

Much of the past twelve years had passed with Nessie and her mother sitting across from each other in the library reading very different books. They had been together in the same room yet worlds apart.

"Me, too." Nessie took a bit bite from her jam-smeared toast. "Oh," she dropped the toast back to her plate, where fruit juice would make is soggy, and grabbed at her gown's buttons, "would you like to see?"

Spoon clattering, Mother held her hands up and turned her head away, making sure to put eyelids and hands between her eyes and Nessie. "Good heavens, no! I do not want to see it."

"Well, why not?" Nessie's elbows sagged from their active posture. "It's a medical marvel."

"Yes, but," deeming it safe to turn back around, Mother sniffed before going back to her oatmeal, "it's also an oddity that is best kept unknown."

What? That wasn't how Nessie saw it. She wanted to tell everyone. To scream it from the decks of airships flying over the town. She was thrilled. She wasn't dying anymore; this piece of strange and amazing technology was giving her a second chance at life.

It was beautiful.

And temporarily full of puss, but no one needed to know that.

Dana entered from the hall, the pistons in her legs making the usual hisses, sounds that made Nessie feel at ease and safe. Her knight was here. "I was thinking of going to the market today. Would you like to come with me?" She stood awkwardly on the opposite side of the long dining table.

While Nessie could go outside, she hadn't actually gone very far. The furthest she'd dared was out onto the back patio for tea one afternoon. And even so, she'd spent the time with her nose in a book. It was lucky that Dana had come around to fetch her before she'd gotten a sunburn.

Granted, even a sunburn was exciting to Nessie.

But while Nessie had barely ventured outside, Dana had been into town many times since Nessie's surgery. She'd been a regular errand-runner for the Ailey household. The cook and housekeeper had even taken to giving their fetching lists to her.

"I do hope you're not going into town dressed like that." Mother scoffed, keeping her eyes on her oatmeal.

Rolling her eyes, Dana shifted the top hat that was under her arm. "I am," she replied with the same almost-resentment she always did.

Nessie thought she looked grand. She wore a dark-brown vest over a creamy, white men's-cut shirt with a pair of khaki-brown tailored shorts.

At one point, Nessie had asked about current fashion; after all, she'd have to adhere to it once she left her house. It turned out that women did not tend to wear shorts; in fact, it was frowned upon. Dana did it because the mechanisms in her legs needed to stay cool and dry, and everyone knew that all skirts did was get hot and muggy underneath.

Honestly, Dana's reasoning could've been 'because I want to' and Nessie wouldn't have had a single word to say in disagreement. Nessie thought shorts were the way to go.

"You want me to go into town with you?" Nessie picked at her cubed melon and soggy toast.

Dana bowed deep instead of simply nodding; she was putting on a show for Mother, which was fine. "I do." She straightened back up. "There is a bookstore next to the entrance to the Covered Market. I've looked at the titles in the windows many times, but I've never known which to buy for you."

She thought about buying Nessie books? Really?

Standing in a rush, Nessie almost knocked her chair over instead of only skidding it across the floor. "I'd very much like to go." She pivoted toward the head of the table. "Mother?"

"It would hardly suit someone homebound to deny you a trip out." She flicked her eyes up. "Enjoy your afternoon."

Nessie grinned in ill-hidden excitement.

When Mother flicked her eyes back to her food, she sighed. "Mandy?"

A squat woman with dimples pressed into her full cheeks appeared in the doorway. "Yes, ma'am?"

The household workers kept out of sight, like they didn't exist, yet could be at her mother's elbow in an instant if called. It was frustrating to Nessie. If she called for Mandy or Teresa, no one would be there, but if her mother sniffed her nose out of place, one would hand her a handkerchief.

"Could you take this into the kitchen for me? I think I'm going to head back to my room for a nap." Mother didn't even wait for a reply; she grabbed the toggle switch on the wheelchair and steered it toward the hallway.

"Miss Kettle?" Dana's voice came out more charming that Nessie was used to.

Mandy spun around to look at Dana; a faint blush tinging her cheeks. "Yes, Dr. Blake?"

Doctor? Nessie whirled around to take in Dana's appearance; looking for a clue to something she'd missed. She was a doctor? Not just an assistant?

"Can you see if Madame Dosett or Miss Kidd have any requests from the Covered Market, today?"

"Yes, Doctor." Mandy bowed. "Right away." She scurried off toward the kitchen with the leftover food.

Belatedly, Nessie realized that she took the rest of her fruit and toast in addition to Mother's cold oatmeal. She grumbled at her misfortune.

Dana watched Mandy leave with a smug smile. "She's so cute when she hurries away to do her work and always so chipper."

"I have a feeling that has something to do with you." Nessie raised an eyebrow.

Placing a hand over her chest, Dana pretended to be offended. "I would never." She shook her head to emphasize her irony.

It was nice having Dana around. Everyone seemed to be in a better mood; even mother was having fun chastising her. It was nice that they could all get a small dose of social interaction that was nothing like the interactions they'd taken part in over the last dozen years.

"Well, you'd best get dressed if you plan to go."

"Oh, right, dressed." Nessie felt nauseous; it derived equally from giddiness and anxiety. She hadn't been expected to be publicly presentable in years. What if she didn't have a dress that fit?

That was unlikely since she had gotten new dresses only a month ago from her cousin in Nouveau Pays. They weren't really Nessie's colors, but at least they'd fit and not look ancient. She planned her outfit, trudging out of the room in small steps.

She'd wear the yellow linen day dress that showed her shoulders with the large sunhat she'd gotten from her mother's closet when she was ten. And maybe the white leather corset if she didn't have to lace it too tight. She'd put on her pearls and take her golden, leather satchel – so she could carry books.

Then it dawned on her. "I don't have any shoes." She turned to look at Dana.

Dana only shrugged. "Don't look at me. I don't even wear shoes."

Swiveling on the heel of her foot, Nessie took off in the same direction Mandy had. "Hey, Mandy? Do you have any shoes I could borrow? It's just for today!"

Nessie stood just inside the guardrail of a steam trolley. She leaned out watching the beginnings of the city grow from beyond the grassy fields. She had to hold her hat on her head to make sure it didn't fly away.

She'd never known just how connected the countryside and the city had become. She still remembered when they'd first moved out to the estate; it had been a day-long drive on a winding dirt road.

This was so much better.

Dana had driven them via steamcar into town, which was nothing more than a little crossroads with a high turn-around repair shop, watering stop, general store, and the trolley station.

Her hair blew around and the hat flapped at her face, making it hard to focus on the disappearing station and commuter lot. Soon, she wouldn't be able to see it at all. If she squinted straight out from the steam-trolley, she could see the winding road disappearing and reappearing around the knolls. She spun around; her hair whipped into her face so she had to spit it away. "So when you said you were going into town, you meant Boston?"

Raising an eyebrow, Dana shifted where she was sitting quietly on the other side of the trolley. It was obviously not as exciting for her. "I don't know what you expected. It's not like I could get any work or collect anything for your attendants back there." She spread her mechanical legs, taking up more space than was strictly necessary. Of course, it didn't matter; they were the only two beings on the trolley.

Nessie crossed her arms over her chest, careful that she didn't smack her right hand on her fluid monitor. She'd done that earlier when she'd struggled to don her newest dress. It hurt; the gauges were fashioned of heavy metal that knocked hard against her knuckles. "I just figured that the town had grown in the last decade." She let her arms drop. "It was disheartening to see that it's still so... bare."

"Podunk."

"Podunk?" Nessie crossed the trolley and sat next to Dana. She tucked her yellow skirt around her legs like Mother had taught her. If only she had shorts like Dana, that would be so much more comfortable, but the dress was nice. It was made of a light material, not too hot.

Dana rattled off, "Dull, rundown, insignificant."

"I get it," Nessie bit out.

"I didn't mean to insult you. You're not dull or insignificant. You're..." Dana paused a moment, looking over Nessie for a long moment, eyes sweeping from her sandal-clad feet to her flapping sunhat, "...endearing."

Nessie laughed. "You're wrong." She managed to say between her breaths. "I'm just as insignificant and dull as anyone else."

They sat in a contented silence. Nessie went back to enjoying the breeze and the smell of fresh air. Sometimes, she'd camp out in front of the filtered fans in the estate, breathing in the new air that pumped into the house, but this was so much better.

Shifting like she was uncomfortable, Dana pulled her legs closer together and stared at her metal feet. They weren't fashioned like normal feet in the least; it was like the designer hadn't even attempted to study the human foot before drawing the plans.

If Nessie had to pick what sort of foot it looked most like, she'd have to say that it looked like the webbed foot of a duck.

"You can't actually believe that you're insignificant, can you?"

Nessie's eyebrows raised at the question. Dana sounded like she was speaking more to herself than to Nessie. Her words were directed at the floor of the trolley car and the volume petered off toward the end.

"You're the daughter of the great architect and engineer, Ray Ailey; the man who perpetually perfected the use of aether generators and mobile energy. You have read more books than most learned men could imagine." She almost looked angry, but it seemed closer to determination or frustration. She made a sharp gesture toward Nessie's chest. "You have a mechanical heart."

"Well, you have four mechanical limbs and you're a doctor, so beat that!"

Dana shook her head. "You don't understand; I'm a doctor because I was fascinated by the procedures that made me mobile." Her face was open; none of the charm from earlier laced into her expression. "All you had to do was be you. Someone loved you so much that you got a mechanical heart." Her eyes trailed down. "And not just any mechanical heart, but the first and only mechanical heart of its kind."

Nessie was stunned. "I'm the first?" She'd figured that mechanical hearts were all the rage, that the rebellious children of the elites were doing it for fun, that there were other people like her.

"You're one of a kind." Dana reached out a hand and placed it on Nessie's upper arm, holding her gently.

It dawned on Nessie that Dana wasn't just gentle around her; she was reverent. As though she was in the front-row-seat to history in the making.

And she was.

Nessie was something epic.

But she wasn't. She was just a girl who'd been in a terrarium for too long. That wasn't a backstory fitting of a hero; that was a backstory fitting for a damsel, and Nessie refused to be a damsel. She was so much more than a prize for some hero to ride in and save.

Raising her chin, Nessie puffed out her chest, except that it sent a twinge through it so she deflated slightly. "That may be so, but that doesn't me that I'm not dull."

Dana pivoted toward her. "You have someone after you."

"You don't know that."

"What do you think that automaton was? A friendly reminder from an old acquaintance?"

"Then why are you taking me into town?" Nessie made a gesture into the direction they were heading. "Shouldn't that be a bad idea?"

"Because I only feel like you're safe if you're with me." Dana's voice was low, a whisper really.

Removing her sunhat, Nessie opened and closed her mouth a few times before concluding that she couldn't honestly disagree. She happened to feel very safe with Dana. She knew Dana would protect her like she was a mother bear with a naïve, helpless, indoorsy cub.

And that wasn't want Nessie wanted. She growled low, leaving the sunhat in her lap, pushing her fingers into her hair, and scraping her nails along scalp; she pressed the heels of her hands to her eyes. "Even if that is true-"

Dana cut her off with a gruff, "It is."

"If it is true," she repeated with more force, "then our goal should be to make me more self-sufficient." She closed her eyes and took a deep breath. She needed to stop running from her problems; otherwise, she'd be stuck in the least-useful archetype for the rest of her life.

"We can stop at the Garrison Supply while we're in Boston."

Nessie nodded, pulling her hands from her hair. She didn't drop them down; instead, she pulled them just far enough away to look over the patterns on her pale palms. Swallowing hard, she smoothed her hair back into a presentable position with one hand and slapped her hat back on with the other.

Turning toward the growing city again, Nessie had to close her eyes so the wind wouldn't dry out her eyes.

So many people.

Nessie hadn't seen this many people in her life, and they hadn't even made it to the city's central station.

People smelled a lot worse than she remembered. Currently, she was pressed between an elderly woman holding a parasol in a way that was stabbing Nessie's side and a man in large, tinted goggles. He wasn't a problem, but he was speaking animatedly with a little girl on his shoulders whose feet swung rhythmically between his chest and Nessie's hat's brim.

Lifting an open hand, Nessie had been annoyed enough. She gauged the swing of the foot, picking the perfect time to strike. When she had it, Dana's hand clasped around her wrist, stopping her from following through.

Sliding in behind her, Dana pressed her body up against Nessie's back, squeezing into the redhead's already-full personal space. Leaning forward and pushing her plush chest into Nessie's shoulders, Dana whispered directly in her ear, "We're almost at our stop. We should move toward the doors."

When Dana spun, she didn't let go of Nessie's wrist. In a fluid movement, Nessie was also spun around and tugged after the doctor. The packed crowd on the trolley seemed to part for the taller of the two women. Women curtseyed and turned away; men tipped their hats to Dana. Dana tipped her hat in return at them, despite the tight squeeze.

Nessie just hoped that Dana didn't let go of her; she might not ever find her again. Although, she could probably ask someone if they'd seen a six-foot, half-automaton woman with a stern expression, and they'd be able to point her in the right direction.

With a jerk, the trolley came to a stop on a bustling street. There were shops lining the road and open gates lined with dark blue flags declaring it the Covered Market.

Women shuffled along the street in pointed shoes with paper bags of produce. A man with greased hair wore a shelf around his neck trying to sell newspapers for a pop coin.

Belatedly, Nessie realized that she hadn't brought any money. She'd brought the satchel, but she hadn't even thought about bringing coin to trade for the books to put in it.

Dana stepped from the car to the light grey pavement below before turning to grab Nessie by the waist, lifting her off of the trolley car, too.

Embarrassed and blushing from Dana's display of strength, Nessie was going to protest, but the trolley car was already lurching forward. She would've fallen had she debarked in her own time. "Thank you." She brushed at her dress.

A man walked quickly past them to Nessie's rear, bumping into her.

Grumbling, Nessie turned in the direction just in time for a woman's pram to brush by her on her other side.

Nessie didn't like all these people. There were too many and none of them seemed to be paying attention to anyone other than themselves. Some were busy looking at their watches; others were reading and walking at the same time. She darted her eyes around, moving from person to person. They all looked the same. They wore the same styles, walked with the same swaggers, made the same faces. It was like they were all programmed by some hive mind.

"Nessie!" Dana grabbed Nessie's face and turned it toward her. "Calm down. It's just people."

"Just? It's a lot of people." She had to speak over the rumble of the crowd and the jangling of the bells on the stores' doors.

Dana looked around, sliding her hands down Nessie's cheeks and neck and settling them on her shoulders.

From that angle, Dana looked very handsome. Her long nose was pointed up with an air of confidence and her chin was raised, exuding regality. Her top hat made a perfect back drop for her defined, expressive features.

Absently, Nessie wondered if anyone had ever looked at her like she was looking at Dana. It was very unlikely; it wasn't as if she'd met many people, especially one shorter than her.

Gently, as always, Dana steered Nessie backward out of the main lanes of foot traffic and into a pocket of empty space in front of a brightly-painted, wooden sign advertising four-scoop sundaes with buyer's choice of four sweet sauces from their extensive forty-five flavor variety.

A part of Nessie wanted to further explore that; she loved sweets. Mother had never approved of her sweet tooth, but she wasn't there to disapprove. And then, Nessie felt guilty about Mother being stuck at home while she was in the city.

Eh, the city wasn't as great as she remembered. It was noisier and more frustrating.

Dana had to step particularly close to her so that a man with a dolly full of wooden crates could pass. He tipped his red newsboy cap. It looked dumb the way it was haphazardly balanced on his afro, but once he'd passed them, Nessie could tell it was part of a uniform; he was wearing a cotton vest and knee-high socks dyed the same color with matching embroidered emblems.

When Nessie turned back, she counted herself lucky that she'd been preoccupied with the uniformed man, otherwise she'd have been staring at Dana's bosom the entire time.

It was a nice, if devastating, view. Nessie wondered how many men had taken notice of it.

"I'm guessing that you're not going to do to well in the Covered Market."

"You don't think so?" Nessie leaned to the side to look in through one of the open gates.

It was packed tighter than the trolley had been. It was packed tighter than when Mother had canned green beans last summer, and they'd been able to live off one jar of that produce for almost three weeks. So many green beans.

Pulling a face that was meant to say 'I think you'd be right but what am I supposed to do?', Nessie looked back up at her companion.

Dana pinched the bridge of her nose and took a deep breath. "How about I drop you at the bookstore and go through the Covered Market for what we need?"

That would give Nessie even more time at the bookstore; it was a dream come true, one of her get-lost-in-a-library fantasies, not one of her escape-to-space ones. "Books?" She may have been drooling.

Clearly relieved, Dana's ruffled stature smoothed into her usual brusque demeanor. "I figured you'd go for that."

The bookstore wasn't huge or otherwise impressive, but it had books that Nessie hadn't read and that was enough for her. It was smaller than the library at the estate; large wooden bookshelves ran up and down the length of the store front, books mashed haphazardly within the spaces.

Dana had dropped her off out front before making a beeline for the Covered Market, promising to be back as soon as possible.

What Dana didn't seem to understand was that she wasn't leaving Nessie alone, per se; she was leaving Nessie with a store full of potential new friends.

Nessie walked up and down the aisles first. She didn't even touch the books; she just looked at them, enjoying the thrill. She raced back to the front of the store.

There were many different sections in the bookstore. The sections most tempting for Nessie were adventure -- filling an entire row of bookcases -- and science fiction -- filling another five.

Rolling from the very edge of her heel to the very tip of her toe, Nessie felt like when she turned twelve and her Papa told her that none of the books in the library were off-limits anymore. It was an immature feeling, but Nessie welcomed it.

She held in her squeal when she found herself standing in front of the first shelf of adventure books. Reaching out like a child who'd been told not to open the biscuit tin until after dinner, Nessie brushed her finger down the spine of one of the books. It was real. It was all real.

In a burst of excitement, she jogged in place twice before settling back down.

Feeling a bit woozy, she decided to sit cross-legged on the floor. She started with the first book in the lower right-hand corner of the bookcase.

Circumspectly, she opened the book. Another trill of excitement buzzed through her when there wasn't an Ailey Library stamp in the front of the book.

"Hello there, Miss, can I help you to find anything?"

Nessie jumped and turned to the newcomer.

The man that had snuck up on her hardly seemed to have the kind of stature that would lend itself to sneaking. He had broad shoulders, made to look even broader by the vest he was wearing, and his long brown hair was pulled into a low ponytail by a dark brown ribbon.

After fumbling around to stand up, Nessie clasped her hands together and let them lie against the front of her day dress. "Hi." She made a short bow.

Raising an eyebrow, the man chuckled. "That wasn't what I'd call a customary greeting." He smiled and his eyes seemed to glow with a good-natured mirth. He wasn't laughing at her, thank goodness. "Are you from abroad?" He loomed forward, expecting a reply.

Instead of replying, Nessie spent the moment staring at him. Could she not even greet people correctly?

Backing down a bit, not being as forward, he gave another friendly smile. "If you are, I would happily show you to our Foreign Releases; it's upstairs. We recently got the next five books in the Dark Skies Series that's been popular in Scotia." He made a vague gesture upward, almost hitting his hand on the ceiling.

"There are more books?"

Laughing again, the man nodded before holding out a hand. "I'm Jameson Worthing; my brother and I own the store. It's a pleasure to make your acquaintance." He sounded a bit like a textbook, using very formal language.

Mother had always taught Nessie to offer her hand for a kiss when she introduced herself. Of course, she'd botched that up; she would've had to introduce herself first. That must've been what Jameson had meant when he said that she hadn't offered a customary greeting.

Nessie stared at the hand for a moment before taking it in her own and pumping it once. "I'm Nessie Ailey. The pleasure is mine." It was nice to shake his hand. He had big hands; his had swallowed her hand up whole.

"Lady Ailey?" Despite that Nessie had let go of his hand, Jameson's hand froze where it had touched hers. "As in Ray Ailey?"

"That'd be my late father." Nessie nodded, it felt weird to say 'late' in that context. It reminded her that he wasn't off on one of his trips; he was really gone. For always.

Jameson offered a deep bow. "May he rest in peace." When he stood back up, his eyes had taken on a glassy quality. "I attended the memorial service; I'm afraid that I didn't offer my condolences to you then." He looked pitiful, kicking himself for failing to do the impossible.

Awkward as ever, Nessie lightly shoved a flat hand to his chest, palm-side down, trying to convey her nonchalance. "Oh, no worries, I wasn't in attendance."

"You weren't in...?" Jameson trailed off.

Deciding that she didn't want to continue that conversation, Nessie spun around to things that wouldn't try to make stunted, melancholy conversation with her. "So, you have quite a few adventure books. Which one is the best?"

"Oh." Jameson turned to the bookcase, too. "You would have to ask my brother." He made another gesture toward the elusive upstairs. He turned over his shoulder and called out, "Jon?"

There was a thudding sound and then a crash.

For a short moment, Nessie was reminded very clearly of the crashing and thudding that had led to the incident with the drone in her house -- and the spider-thing she refused to remember. She shook those fears away. These were nice people, book people; they weren't people to be afraid of.

Offering a little grin as they waited for his brother, Jameson cocked his head to the side, "I don't really read adventure books."

Maybe they weren't nice people.

"But my brother, on the other hand, loves them. I can't get him to read anything else." Jameson shook his head, obviously disappointed in his brother's choice of reading material.

Maybe Jameson wasn't good-book-people, but this Jon seemed to be okay.

A more rhythmic thud pattern came from the back of the store, certainly the sound of feet landing heavily on stairs. From the back of the last row emerged another tall man but not as tall as Jameson. He wore looser clothing that was wrinkled instead of pressed and half of his hair was plastered upward.

It would seem they'd awoken him from a nap.

He looked tired, sporting heavy bags under his eyes and scuffing his toes on the floor.

Nessie was beginning to second-guess the whole bookstore idea.

When his eyes focused on Nessie, his groggy appearance melted away, leaving someone much more approachable in its wake. "Ah." He walked with more fervor. "Lady Ailey, it's a pleasure to meet you in the flesh." He lifted her hand from where it hung limp at her side and brought it to his lips for a kiss. His light stubble scratched at her skin.

It wasn't necessarily unpleasant; she just never wanted to feel it ever again.

Chancing a glance toward Jameson, Nessie saw him roll his eyes.

It made Nessie feel a bit more at ease. If this was just Jon's antics, then she had nothing to worry about.

"Well, since you've got her, I'll go back to the front desk." Jameson bowed and walked away with long graceful steps, but he still spoke to Jon, "And stop using the Walking Man's Radio to listen to erotic fiction." He waved at his brother.

Snickering, Nessie brought her hands to her mouth in a poor attempt to cover it.

Jon's face had gone red and his Adam's apple froze mid bob.

Leaning forward, Nessie leaned up onto her tiptoes and used the hands at her mouth to cup to his ear. "It's okay. I enjoy some of the erotica stations myself." She couldn't believe she'd just said that aloud to another human being. This could backfire so badly, but what was done was done.

Recovering from his embarrassment, Jon lolled his head to one side and sent a skeptic look. "I didn't think erotica was something that elite ladies listened to."

"Well, that's your problem; you think I'm elite." Nessie laughed at her half-joke.

Following suit, Jon barked out a laugh too. It was nice to laugh with someone. It'd been a long time. Jon planted a hand on one of his hips. "So, you're looking for an adventure book, I take it."

Nessie nodded. "You have so many." Her eyes scanned over the entire row of books. "I was wondering where you'd recommend that I start."

Beckoning her with a finger, Jon walked down a few cases. "Well, since you seem to have a fancy for steamier writing, I think you'd enjoy this one." He plucked a blue, fabric-bound book from the top shelf.

The cases were so tall, Nessie couldn't have perused it if she'd tried.

"It's about two spies in Carolinia. One of them is a bit of a ladies' man and the other is a total bookworm." He flips it over, donning an expression akin to reminiscing.

Nessie plucked the book from his hands. "Sounds a bit like you and your brother."

Shrugging, Jon moved one to another book case. "Now, this one is great." He stooped over but came to an abrupt halt to look up at her. "Do you have anything against unconventional couplings?"

What? "What do you mean? Like elite class and lower class?" She squatted next to him, leveling him with a steady stare.

"No, more like..." he faltered over his wording, "more like two men falling in love."

"Is that a thing?"

"Very much so."

"Huh." Nessie's legs went slack, causing her to bounce a little in her squatted position, feet falling flat on the floor and body curving up to distribute her weight evenly.

None of the books in their home library had featured two men or two women together.

She cautiously asked, "Is it a new thing?"

Maybe their library didn't feature it because they hadn't gotten new books in so long.

Searching the spines on the shelf, Jon absently responded, "I don't think so. Aha!" He dug his fingers into the books and pulled out a flimsy, paper-bound book before standing up. "Well, if you're up for it, this is about a band of airship pirates that come across a siren seeking passage to another port to exact his revenge. The brave captain ends up falling for the creature." He offered her the book.

"Ah! That's horrible. Don't sirens eat their victims." She took the book, staring at it in horror.

Jon waved his hands back and forth. "No, no! Lucky for the captain, the siren also falls in love with him." He scratched the back of his neck. "I was trying not to give that part away."

Hugging both of the books to her chest, Nessie nodded. "Okay, okay, sorry. I entrust my reading selection to you." She sent a huge grin. "So, are there any that feature two women?"

Nodding in affirmation, Jon took a step back and pulled out another book. "So, this one is about a copper and a private detective..."

In the end, she selected twelve pops worth of books and was excited to read all of them. Jon had described them with such fervor, that she itched to open their covers.

Jon was definitely good people, and, by the look of approval on his brother's face when she showed him her haul, Jameson was too.

"I can't believe this!" Dana barged through the door to the book shop and grabbed Nessie's wrist.

After collecting a small selection of Jon-approved books, they'd sat in the reading nook in the front of the store. There were two overstuffed, batting-upholstered chairs with well-worn butt-prints in their cushions. It would seem that the Worthing brothers often sat there when the store had no guests.

"What? Why?" Nessie tried to pull away from Dana's grasp, but her mechanical grip had locked on.

Jon rose from his chair, hackles rising. "What's she still doing here? Shouldn't she be off attending to Addler's newest victim?" He shoved the book down on the arm of the chair and balled his hands into fists.

Hissing like a startled stray, Dana put herself between Jon and Nessie. "I assure you that I am just where I need to be." She had a bag of supplies balanced between her other arm and her torso.

"This doesn't make any sense." Jon waved a hand at Dana. "You're supposed to be gone."

"What? So, you have a better chance the next time around?" Dana's grip got tighter. It was beginning to hurt.

Nessie's voice was small compared to their booming. "Dana?"

Jon scoffed. "Chance of what? Messing up weeks, if not months, of meticulously planned work?"

"Jon?" Nessie tried again.

"Yeah, well your plan failed! Lady Ailey is still alive and well."

Alive and well? Was Dana accusing Jon of trying to do harm to her? When would Jon have been able to do that? They'd only met a few minutes ago.

"I'd never try to hurt the Aileys!" Jon growled, lunging forward and getting in Dana's face. "I was trying to protect her."

"Guys!" Jameson's holler broke through Dana's and Jon's banter bubble. "What are you talking about?"

"This," Jon jabbed a hand at Nessie, "is Lady Ailey."

Jameson looked between Nessie and Jon twice, not making the connection that Jon wanted him to make. "And?"

"She's the one that got the heart!"

How did Jon know that? No one knew that. It was need-to-know only, ordered by Mother. She seemed to think that people wouldn't treat the late Ray Ailey and his family the same if they knew.

Nessie hadn't really understood her mother's logic, but, if her surgery was the first of its kind, an experiment, then perhaps people would think Ray Ailey too risky or heartless to buy his inventions, they would think he wasn't a good man because he'd risk his daughter like that.

Little did they know, he was a loving and supportive father.

And Mother insisted that was all people needed to know.

So, how did Jon know about it?

"I thought the heart was for the elder Lady Ailey." Jameson said with an intonation very similar to a small child saying 'oops' after forgetting to complete their homework.

Jon scooted closer to his brother and spoke low and forceful, "No, it was for the younger; I told you that."

Rolling his eyes, Jameson let his shoulders drop in surrender. "Yes, Jon, and you've told me a great many other things when I'm half-asleep at three am, and I don't remember those much, either." Jameson shook his head before turning to Nessie; he seemed intent on ignoring Dana who was still strung up and ready to strike. "I'm glad your surgery went well. It was truly amazing when I heard."

"But how did you hear?" Dana growled. She managed to set the paper bag of groceries on the counter to their left without breaking eye contact with her targets.

Nessie was curious about the answer to that questions, as well.

Bringing her hand up, Dana spread her fingers causing the cap on each finger to flip open. Under each fingertip was a different surgical instrument. She had a blade, a heated cauterizer, a pick, and the blades in her thumb and forefinger looked like a pair of scissor blades.

Jon's hand flew up in surrender. "Holy shit. Okay."

With more cool than his brother had, Jameson also raised his hands in surrender.

Ignoring their raised hands, Dana still advanced, her finger weapons stretched in front of her, heading for Jon's throat. She was still puffed up and angry, still frightened.

That's what Dana was, frightened. And so was Nessie, so, if Dana could use her fear and turn it into bravery then so could Nessie.

Twisting her wrist and yanking down out of Dana's death grip, Nessie took power of her fear. "You can't hurt them." Sliding around Dana, Nessie put herself between Dana's hand o' hurt and Jon, arms spread out to the sides.

Seeing her there, Dana's hand trembled and stopped. "Nessie, get back over here. You don't know these men."

Feeling her pulse quicken in her temples, Nessie stood her ground. "I don't know them, but I know books! And they know books, too! They aren't bad people," she exclaimed. She screwed her eyes shut and fisted her hands into balls. "Let them try to explain!"

When all was quiet for a moment too long, Nessie reopened her eyes enough to peek.

Dana's hand had fallen away. She bent her fingers all at once, and the caps all flipped back into place, once again concealing her surgical tools. She looked like Nessie had kicked her in the stomach instead of simply impeding her torturous aim.

"Alright!" Nessie spun around to glare at the two men. "Sit." She pointed to the chairs. "Then talk."

Taking trepid steps, Jon and Jameson got themselves to their chairs and sat without grace, hands still raised in surrender.

The shared a look before Jon began, "Lady Ailey, I worked for your father. I helped him design that heart."

On the way back to the estate, Nessie managed to grab a seat on the outside of the trolley car, sitting with one leg bent up on the seat with her and turned so she could rest her arms and head on the wide brass rail. She untucked one of her arms and rested it on her chest. "Did you know that my father helped to design this?"

Beside her, on the other side of her bent leg and loosely holding the paper bag full of supplies, Dana sighed. "Lady Ailey, now is probably not the time to talk about it." Her brown eyes flicked around at the other people on the trolley car.

She was right. Nessie slumped. She was also being extremely formal, even more formal than when they'd first been introduced. Nessie didn't like the distance that Dana was putting between them. She shifted her satchel full of books before sliding her arm back into the pile of arms and head she'd made on top of the trolley car's handrail.

"So sorry, but I couldn't help over-hearing. You're the young Lady Ailey?"

Dana grew still next to her and Nessie took in her reaction as she turned to see the man in question.

He was used to the way the trolley car lurched and moved; he stood unwavering nearer to the center of the car without holding any of the handrails. He wore a top hat similar to Dana's except his had a suede pattern on the material, and his long coat was of a matching material. Tipping his hat, he offered a small bow. "It's a pleasure to see you again, Miss Ailey. I met you once when we were both young; I'd be surprised if you remembered."

A lot happened in twelve years. Nessie wasn't sure if she didn't recognize him because he'd grown older or if she'd been too young to remember. If she thought like Dana did, there was the possibility that she didn't recognize him because he was lying. Nessie ignored that possibility. "I'm sorry, sir. You'll have to reintroduce yourself."

"Ah, of course." He plucked at the fingers of his black gloves, pulling just his right glove from his hand and catching it between his elbow and his side. "I'm Benedict

Dickenson. We were once playmates." He offered his ungloved hand.

She cocked her head. Benedict Dickenson had been scrawny; this man showed almost no resemblance to what she remembered of the boy who would play with her at the townhouse's playground when they were toddlers.

In fact, she couldn't be certain if she'd retained her memories or if she was creating memories from the pictures she had seen in an album in the library. When Nessie said that she'd read every book in that library, she meant it; she even had the photo albums memorized.

Dana inserted herself into the conversation, taking his proffered hand. "I'm Dr. Dana Blake; it's a pleasure to finally make your acquaintance Mr. Dickenson." Her smile was tight and her teeth were clenched. "I've seen your work many times, absolutely stunning pieces."

Oh, did he make jewelry? Or time pieces? "Oh, are you an artist?"

Benedict shook his head, letting go of Dana's hand and yet again offering it to Nessie. "I am an inventor. I worked with you father." He offered no smile, but the end of his lips twitched upward.

"You're not the only one," Nessie muttered under her breath.

Nodding along, Benedict leaned back away from them, returning everyone to their appropriate personal spaces. "A lot of people worked with you father; it's true. He kept good relationships with his workers and made sure to know everyone's name by heart." He smiled more than before at the memory. "We worked closely together."

Nessie leaned forward, invested in the conversation. "Oh, like on what? The steam stuff or the aether?"

"Both, and then some." He turned toward the door to the trolley. "We're coming up to my stop. So, I'd best be off. I'll be seeing you on Thursday, though, yes?"

"What's on Thursday?"

The trolley car came to a halt and Benedict moved to get off. With another tip of his hat and a skeptical look, he responded, "Dinner, of course. Your mother said you were looking forward to it during our latest correspondence."

Nessie didn't get a chance to respond, the trolley was already moving again. She sprung up and ran across the car, now with a dwindling number of passengers heading for the outermost stops. She yelled out the window back toward the last stop. "She never said anything to me about it!"

Before she even saw her, Nessie knew that Dana had stood and followed her to the other side of the car. Nessie had memorized the sound of the pistons in her legs.

A bit confused, Nessie's mouth was still open when Dana laid a hand on her shoulder, offering moral support. Nessie jerked her head to look at Dana. "When's Thursday?"

"You set up a date for me and didn't even tell me about it?" Nessie sat at the dining room table, pushing her food around on her plate and pretending that he was hungrier than she was.

After her day in Boston, she'd been looking forward to not going back for a while. Maybe she could send post to the Worthing brothers asking them out to the estate. Honestly, she'd do anything to get out of going back to the city so soon, yet her mother had already minced those plans.

Thursday was the day after tomorrow.

Mother pinched at the spot where her nose met her eyebrow ridge. "Dear, you understand how time gets away from us when we're stuck in here all day." Her hand

dropped from her face and she daintily picked up her fork.
"I would've remembered eventually."

Nessie slapped her fork down on the mahogany tabletop.
"That isn't the point, Mother. Why have you arranged an
outing between Benedict and I? I haven't seen him in ages.
I'm certain that we are very different people than we once
were." She glared at the bread roll on her plate before
snatching it up and tearing it into pieces.

"He's turned into a very nice young man," Mother assured
her.

"Oh, yeah? And how would you know?" As soon as the
words left her mouth, Nessie regretted them, because they
were impolite and disrespectful, but her point still stood.
Mother had been just as cut off from everyone as she had
been over the last decade; how would she know what sort
of a person Benedict Dickenson had turned into?

Humming, Mother almost seemed as though she hadn't
heard her. Nessie was going to repeat the question more
politely, but her mother turned to look at the large painting
of Papa that hung over the other end of the table. "Your
father only ever said good things about him. He was an
apprentice to your father for some time."

She'd never known; he'd never said.

"Did Papa ever talk about Jon Worthing?"

"Only that the boy was too smart for his own good, which made him a smartass."

Nessie laughed. "That sounds about right."

"Did you meet him? Mr. Worthing, I mean?"

"I did." Nessie puffed her chest out, happy when it didn't twinge like the last time, and held her chin up, feeling like she may have accomplished something her mother would approve of. "He owns the bookstore with his brother. He helped me pick out books."

Mother tutted.

"He was very nice." Nessie argued for her friend. "So was his brother, Jameson."

"I'm sure he was, but heaven knows you don't need any more books." Mother pulled her bread roll apart tenderly, just like how she opened envelopes. (Nessie had also shredded her bread roll in the same manner that she opened envelopes.)

Nessie debated whether or not she tell her mother the rest. After a moment's hesitation, she powered onward. "Jameson Worthing also helped. He pointed out some of the better books of poetry. I bought them for you."

Mother's eyes were wide and she sat oddly still, almost expectantly.

Twisting in her chair, Nessie brought the satchel of books around to rest on her lap. She'd already removed any of the books she didn't want her mother to see; they were tucked in the drawer in her nightstand with the others of that variety.

From the satchel, Nessie pulled out two books of poetry. Both were highly recommended by Jameson and one had also gotten an accolade from Jon. He'd said that it had some fantasy and science fiction elements mixed in. "This one also had stuff in it that they think I would enjoy. I figured maybe we could both read it and we could talk about it." She offered a little smile. They hadn't spoken about much of anything for a long time; they'd only ever acknowledged the other's existence when they were both vying for Papa's attention. It was about time she tried to reach out. "Our own little book club."

Picking up the book, Mother looked over its binding before placing it on the table on top of the Ailey Library book she'd been reading while waiting for dinner. "I think that's a great idea."

Nessie smiled.

"But don't think that this gets you out of going to dinner with Mr. Dickenson."

"What?" Nessie protested with a whine. "But, we were getting along and everything was going so well."

Picking up her fork again, Mother used its edge to cut the tender pot roast. "We're getting along well now, but we won't be for too long. Your father left most of his money to our health expenses." She flicked a pointed look at the painting. "He left the company to Mr. Dickenson."

That shocked Nessie. "So, if he chose to, he could freeze us out?" She'd read many legal dramas and economic books.

Mother sighed. "Even if you refuse to court him, I still expect you to go and try to be friends." She turned her pointed look to Nessie. "But, I don't want you to rule out marriage to him yet. He's a good young man. Your father and I had once entertained the thought of bringing him out here to meet you, so you could attempt to court each other that way."

Ugh. Nessie reached over the table and grabbed another bread roll from the basket, intent on demolishing that one too. "So glad that you two valued my opinion."

"Well, at the time you still went on about how boys were slimy, pathetic and gross, so we decided to put it off." Mother's eyes glossed over. "We figured we'd get time to return to the idea, but that, unfortunately, did not happen."

Nessie bowed her head. Here she was getting mad while Mother was hurting over the loss of Papa. She bit her lip.

Honestly, Nessie wasn't sure if she'd outgrown the 'boys are slimy, pathetic, and gross' stage of life yet.

Nessie turned down Dana's invitation into town at breakfast. She'd had enough of the town for the time being and hoped that she could preserve her energy for when she had to play nice with Mr. Dickenson the following evening.

Stretched out over her bed, Nessie was intent on reading. She lay on her stomach and shoved at least four pillows under her chest to raise her up enough to read comfortably.

She made sure the beaded pillow was on the bottom.

Before the procedure, it would have only taken two pillows, and she wouldn't have needed to use the beaded and embroidered pillow at all. It wasn't as if Nessie was a heavy person, but her new heart weighed much more than her old one.

Opening to where she'd left off the night before, Nessie settled in to read.

Jon had made an excellent choice in recommending her the book. It featured two strong female characters; one who was a private detective with a background as a seminary dropout and the other who was a police officer from a reformed mob family.

They were so cool.

After a few pages, Nessie had to look away from the book, squeeze her eyes closed, flutter-kick her feet, and try not to squeal. They were so good at what they did and totally badass. Officer Greenwich reminded her a lot of Dana; she was tall and gruff and beautiful with a snarky attitude and a penchant for punching bad guys. She was probably Nessie's favorite character.

All was going well. Well, all was going well for Nessie. For Officer Greenwich and Detective Rivers, things were going haywire; they'd accidentally begun a shoot-out and were crouching behind a steambuggy.

It was so good.

Nessie's eyes flew across the page; the writing pace was quick and kept Nessie wanting for more with ever line.

Then she flipped the page, and her reading came to a halt over the word 'kiss'.

Her face grew red and she peeked around her room. It was infantile to make sure no one had unexpectedly showed up in her room, but she couldn't stop herself. Biting her lip, she left the book open and flipped over on the bed as she hurried to check out the window and pull her curtains closed.

Giggling a little, she hurried back to the bed, flopping down heavier than she wanted because of the heft of her metal heart and pulling at the chain for the lamp next to her bed. It buzzed to life when the aether began to flow through the light tube behind the sheer lampshade.

She settled back into her book, grinning so wide that her face ached.

For the next two pages, the two characters kissed.

Part of Nessie thought it was highly irresponsible for them to do this during a firefight, but much of her brain activity was preoccupied with the description of the women. Everything was described as soft.

There was no mention of chapped lips or stubble like in the other books Nessie read. There were no angular planes of pecs or washboard abs. There was no clothing ripping or forced movements.

Nessie's blush began to impede her eyesight; she was tearing up from the heat pooling behind her eyes.

And that wasn't the only place where heat was pooling.

When the two characters exchanged words of comradery and returned their attention to the firefight, Nessie had to put the book back down and flop over to her back.

She squeezed her legs together and her eyes shut.

Blood rushed in her ears. Her hands and face felt clammy. A book had never done this to her before. She sucked in a big breath, she expanded her chest to the point just shy of pain. Her giddiness burst in a momentary spell of giggles, writhing on the bed while pumping her hands and arms in the air above her.

Once the wave of excitement passed, she opened her eyes again.

Except that the room was spinning a little. Then her breathing became forced and shallow. Then the rushing in her ears stopped.

Fear trickled into her muddying brain. Fumbling around, Nessie managed to pop open the fluid monitor on her wrist and take out the brass key. With shaking hands, she pulled open the neck of her dressing gown.

She felt like she was choking. Her vision still spun, so she had to slide the key around on the metal plane of her chest before fitting it into the key hole. She gave it one good wind.

It tugged hard in the core of her chest, but the world started to come back into focus. Her head ached; she flopped it back down onto the mattress.

Regulating her breathing, Nessie turned the key until she felt the slightest resistance and stopped, just like how her father had taught her to wind a pocket watch.

Papa had always reminded her of that.

With the danger passed, Nessie left the turnkey in her chest and brought her hands up to her face. She pressed the heels of her hands into her eye sockets and blew out a long, heated breath. That had been scary.

Eventually, her hands fell away from her face and she opened her eyes again. Turning her head, she leveled her gaze with the book lying next to her on the quilt. She breathed in and out two more times before she convinced herself that the episode was over.

Donning a smile, Nessie snatched up the book and brought it to her chest. She held it in front of where the turnkey still rested in her chest and continued to read.

Three hot pages into Officer Greenwich and Detective Rivers' sex scene, there was a quick rap on her door followed by her mother pushing open the door and entering the room.

Nessie scrambled on the bed. Mother hadn't been to her room in years.

"How can you live in this dark room?" She drove her chair over to the windows and opened the curtains. "Is it usually this dark?"

Mumbling into the book she'd pulled in close to her face, Nessie pulled her knees up to her chest, squeezing her legs tight together. "Not usually."

"No wonder you take Vitamin D supplement."

"You take Vitamin D supplement, too."

"Yes, but I at least try to get it the natural way." With the windows opened, the sun beamed in through the tinted panes.

Squinting at the bright light, Nessie groaned and turned away.

Mother roved back around the bed and grabbed at her leg, shaking it. "Come on. Get up! Tonight's your date." She reached over to the lamp and tugged on the chain to turn it off. It glowed for an extra moment before it dulled. "I wanted to talk to you at dinner last night, but you didn't come out. The housekeeper had to bring you your dinner in here."

At the mention, Nessie flicked her gaze over to the tray still laden with quiche and potatoes.

"Did you read all night?" Mother shook her head. "You should've slept; tonight is very important." She tutted. "I do hope you got to a good stopping point." She steered away from the bed and toward the armoire, pulling open the drawers and rifling through their contents.

Nessie didn't dare tell her that she'd spent the last three hours reading and rereading the latest sex scene. She paused at the end each time to hum and squeal and wiggle her toes.

It was just too good, but she put the book down -- closed.

"Now," having rifled through her drawers, Mother parked the chair next to the settee and pulled her cane from the tube that Papa had welded to the chair's frame for that exact purpose, "let's get your clothing sorted." She pushed up to stand.

Rushing over, Nessie spotted her mother while she hobbled to the settee and sat down.

Once sitting, Mother shimmied her shoulders, shaking off her struggle like a dog shook off rain. "How about the gown your uncle sent?"

Nessie scoffed, "How about not." It was a formal blue satin piece with uncomfortable boning up the torso and a hoop-skirt. "I can hardly walk through a door in it."

Huffing, Mother tapped the tip of her cane to the floor; whether she was frustrated at her daughter or just thinking, Nessie was unsure. It was only just turning noon and dinner wasn't until four-thirty. Nessie was pretty sure that all of the fussing could wait for a few more hours.

"I could show you the dresses that Cousin Talley sent from Nouveau Pays." She stepped toward the hanging section of her armoire. "The yellow one from Tuesday?" She grabbed the skirt and swung it outward from the rest of the clothing, holding it in front of her so her mother could see. "It was one of them." She picked through the rest of her wardrobe looking for a matching blue dress with white embroidery, then for the white dress with the floral embellishments.

"Oh, that one."

"The white?"

"Yes. You'll look lovely in it." Mother's head had relaxed to the side and her lips had turned up into a little smile.

Nessie looked over the white one. She turned a wary look toward her mother. "Are you sure? Don't you think I'll stain it?" She ran her hands over the thin fabric. The dress would drape over her loosely but come in to an embroidered collar and cuffs. At least the white leather corset would work with it.

Her mother sniffed her nose and tilted it into the air. "A lady doesn't worry about stains; they eat their food with grace and poise."

Narrowing her eyes, Nessie deadpanned, "Then I mustn't be a lady."

"Pish. Just be careful." She leveled her chin again and looked over the dress, scanning up it, then past it to Nessie's face. "You will look so beautiful."

Nessie was immediately reminded of Dana paying her the same compliment.

From her mother, the compliment didn't illicit the same feelings. She still didn't believe it, but, when Dana had said it, her entire body felt a little lighter, tingly even. When he mother said it, she felt like a proper woman, like she looked like what her mother expected, not like herself.

It was as if Dana's compliment had meant that Nessie's personal, unique appearance was pretty and that her mother's compliment meant that Nessie had finally found a way to fit the normal definition of beauty.

Nessie found herself preferring Dana's version.

It stirred something in her. It felt similar to when she had to wind up her heart, but it was lower in her abdomen, between her hips.

Blushing, she turned her face to her armoire and dug in to get the hanger for the white dress.

Misinterpreting the flush, Mother gave a light snicker. "It's nothing to be embarrassed about. You've grown into a stately young woman."

Crossing the room, Nessie pulled at the golden rope holding one of the four-poster-bed's curtains to the side. She pulled it with her to the halfway-point of the bed and then hurried to change behind it. Mother had seen her bare before, after all, the woman was her mother, but Nessie hadn't been undressed in front of her in years; it was unsettling.

Of course, she'd been undressed in front of a bunch of nurses for almost a month.

And one Jon Worthing.

She still couldn't believe that Jon had pretended to be a nurse.

Even with his good intention of protecting Nessie and the mechanical heart, it was still a bit creepy.

She pulled the soft fabric up over her shoulders and fastened the two buttons of the collar at her neck. Stepping out from behind the curtain, she made a small spin for Mother, showing off the flow of the material where is swung around her in rippling waves of white.

"It's so pale that you look like you have color in your complexion."

Nessie rolled her eyes.

It would seem that her mother was back to her usual back-handed compliments, but her smile was true. "It's perfect."

Nessie was enjoying the garden when Dana came to collect
her.

"Are you ready to go?" Dana wore a different pair of
shorts; these ones were black with a grey pinstripe. She
had a matching top hat at her elbow.

Shaking her head, Nessie turned back to the flowers. She
reached out and ran a hand over the petals of one of them.
"Mother's been hysterical for most of the day. She helped
me pick out my dress. She did my hair."

Dana let out a puff of breath. "I was wondering why your
hair was like that."

It was piled on her head into a mass of wispy, red curls. It
didn't look bad, per se, but it definitely didn't look natural,
which was the look that Nessie preferred. When she shook

her head, the weight of it made her head wobble on her neck more than it usually did.

Nessie said, "I don't like it" at the same time that Dana said, "You're beautiful."

With her mouth open and her eyes blinking rapidly for a moment, Nessie was struck silent.

Stepping closer, Dana used a metal finger to lift a stray lock back to her head. "I'm sorry that you don't like it."

Rushing to reply, Nessie stammered out, "If you like it, then I like it."

"That's not a very good reason to like it." Dana cocked her head to the side and leveled a somewhat disappointed stare at Nessie. "I want you to like it for yourself."

But Nessie just wanted Dana to like her.

Grimacing down at the flowers in her hand, Nessie brought her other hand to her chest. She could feel the hard metal through the thin material of the dress, just above the leather waist-corset's edge. "That's the problem, isn't it?" She shook her head. "I can't do anything for myself."

They stood in silence.

Nessie brought her chin back up, looking at Dana for a moment before deciding to close her eyes. She didn't want to see the woman in front of her; she wanted to see herself. She wanted to know what she wanted, not what everyone else wanted for her. She let out a disappointed sigh.

"You *couldn't* do anything for yourself."

"What?" Nessie opened her eyes and her vision with Dana. She was warm, varying shades of brown and tan, so opposite of Nessie's cold and pale palette.

Dana took a step closer. "Before this," she tapped a finger to Nessie's metal chest, "you couldn't do anything, but now...," she trailed her eyes up to Nessie's face and her finger followed suit, gliding along the fabric, then along the column of Nessie's throat, then to her chin, catching there, "now, you're learning about yourself. What you like; what you don't like."

Wanting to hold onto the moment, Nessie grabbed a fistful of Dana's shirt, a men's cut oxford.

"So, tell me Nessie, what do you want?" Dana tilted her head to the side, awaiting an answer.

Swallowing hard, Nessie tried to swallow down the lump in her throat.

She wanted to not be so scared all the time. She wanted to not court Mr. Dickenson. She wanted to stand up to her mother more.

More presently, she wanted to talk. She still hadn't managed to move the lump from her throat.

Surging forward, Nessie connected her lips to Dana's. Her other hand fisted another part of Dana's shirt.

Dana stayed perfectly still.

After a moment, Nessie pulled away, landing heavy on her heels.

When she left the taller woman, Dana's eyes were wide and her pupils were following her retreat. Her facial features were spread in surprise.

This was bad. Nessie had done this all wrong. Life wasn't one of her storybooks. Dana wasn't Officer Greenwich and Nessie was definitely not Detective Rivers. None of the characters in that book were Nessie. She was more like the nameless princess in her childhood fairytale novels.

Nessie turned away from Dana even though it felt embarrassing and hurt somewhere beyond the metal in her chest. "We should be going if we plan to get there for

four." She flicked at one of the flowers on the bush before
walking away.

Never once during the journey into town, which was almost an hour, did Dana mention that Jon would be joining them for dinner. Of course, neither of them had spoken, but this sort of disregard for sharing information was more fitting to Mother than to Dana.

Benedict was glaring at Jon. "Why is he here?" His voice was stern.

Crossing her arms, Nessie found herself on the defensive. Jon was good people; what did Benedict have against him? Papa had only ever said nice things about the two men.

"I'm here to make sure you don't die in that thing." Jon gestured to the airship.

"But you hate flying."

"I hate the idea of you dying more than I hate flying."

"That almost sounds like a compliment."

"Maybe it almost is."

Taking them each by the back of their pressed collars, Dana steered them up the ramp to the airship's main deck. She rolled her eyes in response to their bickering.

Nessie almost snickered.

They were like brothers, or, if she considered the 'unconventional pairings' that Jon had introduced her to, perhaps they were bickering like a married couple. The new possibilities were endless.

A well-dressed host greeted them at the door to the dining area. "Good evening. May I have your name?"

"Benedict Dickenson," Benedict said pleasantly.

Jon sneered and pulled away from Dana's hold. "More like Dick-Dick."

Leaning over, Nessie flicked him in the neck for being rude.

"Ah, right this way." The host turned and led them to a table near a large porthole. "This is for the Lady Ailey and Mr. Dickenson." He turned to Dana and Jon, "As for your guests, we have another table for them over here; follow me."

Shoving his hands into his pocket, Jon let himself be led away. Dana sent Nessie a blank look before following.

The host led them across the room. They weren't near a porthole, so they wouldn't get to see the view.

"Good. From there, Jon can pretend he's on the ground." Benedict pulled out a chair for her. "Please, sit. It's been a while."

Nessie pulled out the other chair and sat herself down. "I don't mean to be rude, but I want to make sure that you understand that I do not intend to court you." She laced her fingers together and set them on the table ahead of her. "I want to become friends."

Blinking once, Benedict nodded and sat in the chair. "I'm glad that you were forward with me. I hope you'll approve of me being forward with you."

This made Nessie nervous, but it was probably best. She gave a nod and tried to maintain a serious expression. She wanted Benedict to know she was strictly business.

His cool expression morphed into a slight smile. "I did not intend to court you either."

Nessie sagged with relief. "Oh, thank god."

Chuckling, Benedict waved over a passing waiter. He ordered a drink for himself before nodding to Nessie and allowing her to order her own drink. She ordered a strawberry daiquiri. It was only when the waiter left that she realized that she may have wanted to order a less stainable drink.

The airship filled with other guests from Boston's elite, upper class. Some people came over to speak to Benedict or introduce their dates to him. He was a regular celebrity. Sometimes, Benedict would introduce Nessie to them; most times, he wasn't given the chance. The other people didn't seem to care who Nessie was.

Nessie didn't mind. People weren't her thing anyway.

She busied herself with looking through the filling chairs to see Dana and Jon. Half the time, Dana looked annoyed and, the other half, amused. Jon was steadily turning a green color.

It was concerning.

"He hates flying."

Startled by the direct conversation, Nessie turned wide eyes back to Benedict.

"Last month, we had to fly out to Providence to meet with the other manufacturing facility out there. He spent the entire time listening to a Walking Man radio." Benedict shook his head. "His humming was very annoying."

By then, they were waiting on their appetizers. An announcement came over the analog p.a. system, "We will be ascending shortly."

Nessie bounced a little in her chair, looking forward to seeing the city from above. "You don't seem to like Jon very much. Is there a reason?"

Propping an elbow on the table, Benedict deposited his chin into his palm. "He's a ladies' man." He slid narrowed eyes across the room to where Nessie knew Jon and Dana were sitting. They'd since gotten drinks; Dana hadn't touched her water, but Jon had already chugged his cider. Absently, Benedict added, "I am not a ladies' man."

It certainly seemed true enough. Jon was very talkative, all grins and charm, while Benedict was more awkward and subdued. Nessie didn't know what to say next; she wasn't even sure if Benedict had properly answered her question.

"So, now that you're able to explore and get out of the house, I want to extend an invitation to Ailey Industries' Executive Council's meetings. As the owner of forty-three percent of the company's stock, you still own the company and have a say in its activities."

"Only forty-three? Mother said we owned over half."

"You do. Your name is on forty-three percent and your mother's name is on another ten. When she dies, hopefully no time soon, you'll inherit her share, as well." Benedict explained easily.

The appetizers came out on half-size automatons. They were mostly wheel, balancing trays gyroscopically over a metal scaled ball. Benedict lifted the tray of bruschetta from the automaton and set it on the table.

Over at Dana and Jon's table, they'd ordered at least three plates of appetizers, though Nessie couldn't tell what they were.

"He must know that we're dining on the company's dime." Benedict shook his head in resignation.

Dana took a big bite of one of the items.

Nessie reached over the table and placed a hand on Benedict's arm in sympathy. "I'm sure Dana is equally at fault."

"In my limited experience with Dr. Blake, I've found her to be a polite, formal person." Benedict argued. "Over the years I've known Jon, I've learned that he is the exact opposite."

Laughing a little, Nessie replied, "With more time, you may find that Dana isn't as civil as she first appears."

"Is that so?" Benedict picked up a piece of bruschetta and took a bite. He turned away from Jon and Dana to look out the porthole. "You can see the factory from here."

Nessie jerked her chair closer to the window. "Where?"

He pointed at a large building with smoke stacks billowing steam.

"I'd love to take a tour someday." She sat back in her chair. "I am the owner after all."

Still looking out the window, Benedict seemed to be lost in something different than the vision of a city below.

"Is it bad?" Nessie picked up and inspected her own piece of bruschetta.

"Hm?" Benedict snapped back. "Sorry, is what bad?"

"The factory."

"No. Your father was a very good people person. When Boston edited their labor laws, Mr. Ailey hadn't had to change anything in the factories. He'd already eliminated as much of the pollution as he could. He'd already made the working conditions as safe as possible. He'd already standardized the work week. He was ahead of his time." Benedict gave a long sigh; so much air came out that Nessie was afraid that his lungs would be inside out. "I have no clue how I'm supposed to follow in his footsteps."

The idea of overseeing so many people's livelihoods was frightening. Nessie never wanted to have that job.

"I suppose that's why your father made Jon vice-president."

The pieces fell into place. Nessie could see a lot more of the picture. Two apprentices who fought like siblings were left in charge of the company. And then there was their teacher's blood-and-bone child, thrown in just for the fun of it.

Nessie let that all sink in.

"Ah! Our meals are coming out." Benedict turned in his chair when the rumbling of the little ball automatons started to reverberate through the hull of the ship. They came out of the far swinging doors.

Most of the other patrons watched in amazement at their approaching food.

The rumbling stopped when the little drones paused at the tables. Beneath the sounds of the patrons cooing, Nessie heard the tell-tale sound of Dana's piston legs, but after a glance in that direction, she found Jon and Dana excitedly pulling plates from their automaton.

Worry flooding her, Nessie jumped up, startling Benedict where he was moving their entrees to the table.

"Is something wrong?"

Nessie couldn't speak; the best she could manage was a fervent nod.

From the same doors that the cute rolling automatons had come through came a full-sized one. It was the same as the one that had broken into her room, same as the one that had given birth to the spider monstrosity that gave her nightmares she'd prefer to forget.

With a shaking hand, Nessie pointed where it approached.

"Nessie, look out!" It was Jon's voice that cut through the crowd.

Shortly after, Dana's arms grabbed Nessie and moved in front of her, shielding her. "Are you okay?"

Nessie nodded.

From around Dana's shoulder, Benedict stood. From his coat sleeve, he pulled out something that looked like a police baton crossed with Nessie's aether lamp. He turned a dial on its solid, metal end and the device buzzed to life. It crackled with the aether energy.

Jon was the first to confront the automaton. He kicked at its torso's outer shell, breaking it off in one go. "It seems I've gotten better at that."

Even with its inner workings accessible, the automaton still functioned perfectly well.

Where Jon had swiveled to grab a vase off the table, probably to shove into its chest cavity to deactivate it like Nessie had, the drone grabbed his arm and threw him into a table across the room.

With that destructive move, the frozen patrons jerked into action, running away from the fight.

"Move out of the way!" Benedict yelled at people who kept getting between him and the drone. "It's not after you. With its miniscule programming, it doesn't even see you."

But people weren't listening; people were panicking.

Luckily, Nessie was past the panicking stage. She pushed around Dana and yelled out, "Everyone to the other side of the room," drawing everyone's, including the drone's, attention.

As if they'd simply been waiting for an order, the frenzy of people rushed to comply. The tables were devoid of people save where Jon was groaning next to one toppled over.

Benedict nodded over his shoulder. "Thank you."

The automaton took the moment of distraction to extend its arm and spread its fingers very wide. Just like Dana's, the caps of the fingers flipped back to reveal surgical tools. With its newest weapons drawn, it charged at Nessie.

Mid-stride, Benedict lunged at the automaton, thrusting the charged aether-baton to the drone's side. The aether's buzz traveled through the entire machine, and, when it's foot met the ground, it crumpled into a heap.

Struck still with fear, Nessie trembled in place. "What about the spider?" She whispered.

"The spider?" Benedict turned off the baton and put it back went to put it back in his sleeve.

Jon had made his way back over, limping a bit and cradling an arm to his chest. He swiped the baton from Benedict's hand and put it on the table instead. "I can't believe you're still carrying that thing." He growled. "That shit could kill you."

Rolling his eyes, Benedict dropped his arms to his side in resigned defeat, "It hasn't killed me yet."

Shaking his head in disbelief, Jon turned to the two women in their company. "The spider was probably zapped, too. I wouldn't expect it to survive the pure aether that thing gives off."

It was still killing her mother decades after an accident; Nessie had to agree with Jon, on both of his points.

Benedict looked between them all. "What spider?"

The employees moved the guests to other rooms. Some of them had fainted. Others were demanding to land. Still others were demanding their food or refund.

Once Jon had deemed the automaton safe, that it didn't still have any residual aether buzzing through it, Benedict knelt to examine it. "This would be easier if I had my tools," he grumbled, peeling back the outer shell of the automaton's head.

Dana knelt next to him; holding out her hand, she spread her fingers. Her tools became visible when the covers flipped back.

"I knew I'd seen that before." Jon pointed at the drone's hand, where it had was basically identical. "You threatened me and Jameson the same way."

"Jameson and I," Benedict corrected automatically.

"Whatever, college boy." Jon kicked at the automaton's arm. "So, that can't be a coincidence."

Nessie glared at Jon. What did he think he was implying?

Plucking the instruments from her fingers and handing them to Benedict, Dana agreed, "I had the same thought when I saw the three that attacked the Ailey Estate."

"Three?" Nessie yelped in surprise. She'd only seen the one.

Jon snickered. "I thought they'd followed me there. We had two attack the workshop the day before. Ben zapped those two, as well. Those ones either didn't have spiders, or, more likely, the spider had been disabled by the shock too." He chuckled, throwing his head back, "Imagine my surprise when I gutted one with a wrench at your estate and a freaky spider thing crawled out of a hatch in the back of its head."

Feeling clammy from all this discussion of the evil spider-things, Nessie shivered. "Well, coming out a back hatch is better than digging its way through its own head to burst out the front of its face."

Dana laid her free hand on Nessie's thigh, commiserating.

Making a disgusted noise, Jon shuddered. "That sounds horrifying."

"I found the product information." Benedict held up a piece of metal from the inside of the drone's head. He swiveled it in the light, trying to read it. "Does anyone have a magnifying glass?"

"Nope," Nessie chirped.

Dana shook her head. "I don't use that for my work."

Reaching out a hand, Jon motioned for Benedict to pass it to him. "I told you all that work with aether would mess up your eyes."

Benedict huffed but handed it over.

"It only has a date stamp and a production number."

"What's it's production number?"

"Three of eight."

Benedict turned away from the automaton, letting if fall to the floor with a crash. "Okay, how many have he already disabled? I zapped two at the workshop." He pointed at Nessie.

As a question, Nessie pointed at herself before responding. "I took one out in my room with an empty anesthetic canister." Nessie swiveled her hand on her arm to point at Dana.

In the background, Jon congratulated her, "Nice."

"I took one out by slamming a door on its head." Dana added.

"Nicer." Jon repeated before adding his own, "And, like I said before, I took out one with my wrench."

Holding out his fingers, Benedict nodded. "Then this one. That means we've taken out six of them, leaving two more."

Dana swallowed. "They'll probably be waiting for us when we land."

"In that case," Benedict nodded to himself, "we need a plan."

After they explained the situation -- and Nessie, Jon, and Benedict took an impromptu vote resulting in the use of company funds to pay for half of the damages -- the staff of the airship was kind enough to lend them some conductor cord and kept everyone in their new accommodations.

And, like they'd suspected, drones were waiting for them when the staff let down the ramp.

But, instead of two, there were three.

"Why are their three of you?" Jon yelled.

Dana and Benedict turned identical, incredulous looks in his direction.

Nessie was hidden just inside, pressed into the wall next to the door, hidden from the enemy. She was in charge of the aether generator. They had a plan.

Peeking out but remaining in the shadow of the wall, Nessie could see most of the scene. Where she could see two whole drones and half of the other, they looked identical. In sync, they all cocked their head to the side.

"That's because one of us used to be human." It was only one tinny voice, but Nessie couldn't tell which one said it.

In the moment that Nessie devoted some of her brain to determining the human one, they surged into action, revealing the weapons in their fingers and pumping the pistons in their arms and legs into a run.

Dana, Benedict, and Jon each took one length of conductor cord tied to their belt loop. Jon kicked his drone's feet out from under it and managed to tie the cord around it, disabling it.

The tinny voice mocked them, "Still haven't got me."

Dana landed a punch across her drone's face, but Benedict wasn't having as much luck. His drone had wrestled him into a headlock.

Turning to Nessie, Jon smirked, "In that case, let 'er rip." He jumped up and backed away from the cord.

Nessie counted along the switched on the side. Jon's chord was connected to the third switch. She flipped it. The aether generator buzzed to life, sending a glowing, crackling dose of aether down the exposed conductor cord.

The drone wrapped in the chord crackled and crumbled.

With it disabled, Nessie flipped the generator back off.

Jon gave a triumphant holler.

Benedict managed out a mangled, "Glad you bested yours, feel like helping me out?"

"Nah," Jon deadpanned, "you seem to have it covered."

The tinny voice yelped in pain when Benedict haphazardly connected his elbow to his drone's side.

Dana, who was standing a foot away from her drone in a standoff, grinned. "Well, I didn't make you screech, so..." She reached behind her for her conductor cord. She made a quick loop of it and lassoed the drone. "Go for it, Nessie."

Getting excited, Nessie counted the switches and flipped the fourth one.

But she'd miscounted; that was the wrong one.

The cord attached to Benedict and the human-drone began to glow; Nessie immediate turned it off, but the section of glow continued down the cord. She yelled out, "Benedict!"

"Ben!" Jon sprinted toward him.

Dana struggled where she'd tightened her cord loop around her drone. "Nessie, flip mine."

Lip quivering, Nessie counted the switches twice to make sure she found the fourth one, then flipped it on. The glow followed the correct cord and Dana let go in time for the zap to only hit the drone.

With the two drones down, Nessie turned her attention back to Benedict. The aether shock had taken down the human-drone, but it had also hit Benedict.

Jon skidded to a stop next to the heap. Without regard for any residual aether, he pulled Benedict out from the collapsed drone's grip. "Ben?"

"I told you that pure yellow aether didn't affect humans," Benedict muttered where he was pressed to Jon's chest.

Rolling his eyes, Jon made a show that he was irritated instead of relieved; however, his body relaxed and sagged into the ground, still cradling a groaning and hoarse Benedict. "The bastard's fine."

Nessie sighed. And lucky for her, no one was blaming her.

If she were Jon and Benedict were Dana, she'd be throwing blame without question.

From behind her, a drone's arms wrapped around her torso, squeezing tight. For a moment, Nessie fought it, trying to get away, but she stopped when she heard a faint sob and a tear hit her shoulder, immediately soaking through her thin dress. "I don't know what I'd have done if that was you."

Chuckling without sound, Nessie wriggled to turn around in Dana's arms. "I don't know what I would've done, either." After a moment, she added, "Though, it would probably be less violent than your solution." She laughed aloud at her own joke.

Dana didn't laugh; she just hugged tighter.

Patting her back awkwardly, Nessie snuggled into the hug.

With the danger passed, she wanted to curl up in her bed and sleep. In fact, she was almost nodding off there in Dana's arms; perhaps she'd rather sleep there.

When Nessie pulled away and Dana deemed it appropriate to let her go, Jon had pulled Benedict up from the ground, supporting him on one side. "Hey, where's tin man?"

Jerking her head, Nessie noticed the empty spot where the human-drone had been.

Benedict's hoarse voice cut through the silence, "It really was human."

"I heard all about it on the radio," Mother scolded, "I cannot believe you would put yourself in that kind of danger."

Nessie rolled her eyes. "It wasn't like I knew we would be in danger there. I didn't even know the drones had attacked Benedict and I separately."

Taking a short pause, Mother's expression grew expectant, her mouth hanging open a little. "You're on a first name basis with Mr. Dickenson?"

"Well, when you almost die with someone, it usually makes you friends." Nessie explained, fiddling with her fingers in her lap.

Under the table, something nudged her foot.

Across from her, Nessie saw the minute smile on Dana's face. The nudge came again. It was Dana's foot. Nessie smiled back and returned it.

"Well, I say!" Mother put a hand over her heart, worried and frazzled over the incident. So worried and frazzled that she hadn't even postponed the conversation until morning. "This is why you need a man." She threw her arms in the air.

"It's okay, Mother. I have Dana."

Mother shook her head so hard that her chair shook. "No, don't you see? You need someone to protect you. Someone to take care of you, a breadwinner." She clasped her hands on the table in front of her. "This," she banged them on the table in cadence with her words, "is why," bang, "I'm trying," bang, "to marry," bang, "you off!"

Stealing courage from Dana who always exuded it in excess, Nessie stood abruptly from her chair. She puffed up her chest and spoke with emphasis, "It's okay, Mother. I have Dana." Nessie leveled her mother with a steely glare.

Looking back and forth between Nessie and Dana, Mother's mouth hung open. "What?" She kept looking back and forth but her frequency slowed.

Nessie wanted to stand up to her mother.

Marching around the table, Nessie grabbed Dana's hand and entwined their fingers. With as much force as before, Nessie repeated, "It's okay, Mother. I have Dana."

In her wheelchair, Mother sat dumbfounded, mouth hanging entirely open.

Honestly, Dana's expression wasn't that different.

Sniffing in through her nose, Nessie kept on. "Now, we've been through a bit of an ordeal, so we're going to bed." She tugged Dana up to follow her to the doorway. Once in the doorway, Nessie looked over her shoulder. "If I were you, I wouldn't go barging into my room in the near future."

And with that, Nessie exited the room, pulling Dana along behind her. It was quiet except for the sound of Dana's pistons and the occasional sound of metal clinking together.

Once in her room, Nessie thought she might collapse, her borrowed courage dwindled to nothing.

Luckily, Dana caught Nessie between her body and the closed door and returned her courage to her using mouth-to-mouth.

Author's Note

Hello everyone! I hope you enjoyed this fic as much as I do! Although, I'll be the first to admit that I probably should've started writing it earlier than 3 days before the deadline for submission. Oh well.

A bit about myself, I am an agender individual, hence the penname MxKnowitall (though this is written under Morven Moeller), who identifies as asexual and panromantic. I am a Mathematician by education and a teacher by experience.

Some of my other creative endeavors include fanfiction, fanart, original writing and art, card games, and role play games. I started writing original content at the prime age of three and started publishing my work informally at 13 and formally at 16.

If you liked this book, please review it on Amazon or let me know on another site like Facebook, Tumblr, Archive of Our Own, or Instagram!

A peek into

the *rough* beginning of book two

of 'A Brass Book' series,

One Eye or Another

Benedict couldn't believe the nerve of these people. Everyone sported over-the-top outfits for the Public Gala. He and Nessie had attended together under the direction of Nessie's mother, Lady Katherine Ailey. Supposedly, it was good for their image.

Although she was probably right, Benedict didn't understand people's fascination with heterosexuality. It wasn't as if that was the only way things fell into place.

Sometimes women fell in love with women. Sometimes men fell in love with men.

Sometimes apprentices fell in love with their pseudo-brothers and kept it secret for over seven years.

When an automaton waiter passed, Benedict took one of the tube-like glasses of ale. He needed to be more inebriated if he expected to survive the evening.

Speaking of inebriated, Jon waltzed over without a partner. "Benny," he whined, "will you dance with me?" His cheeks were flushed and he was practically bending himself in two backward to make a pouty face at Benedict.

"No." He took a long chug of ale.

Flipping around and righting himself, Jon took one of Benedict's hands, "How about now?"

Furrowing his brows, Benedict tried to repress the emotions stirred by their touching fingers. "What exactly changed in the five seconds between you asking the first and second times?"

When Jon was drunk, he was annoying. He got flirty with Benedict and plucked on all his heartstrings, like he was one of the pulley-mechanized experiment dolls they kept in the back room at the workshop because they were creepy.

"I dunno, you took a swig of your drink and had a 'why the hell not?' sort of look on your face."

"You're mistaken; that was my 'why the hell would I do that?' expression."

Shrugging, Jon attempted to take a drink from Benedict's glass, leaning drunkenly on his shoulder.

Holding the glass out of his reach, Benedict scanned the crowd for Dr. Blake, Jon's handler for the evening. She often pretended that she didn't enjoy accompanying the Ailey Industries' vice-president, one Jonathan Worthing, to events such as there, but Benedict had learnt that the collected and mature outer appearance of the doctor didn't always match her true feelings.

Sometimes, he'd even found her bracing one of her metal hands on Jon's shoulder while she doubled over laughing at one of his inane puns.

"Oh, hi, Jon." Nessie swept into place next to Benedict; she was a vision in the outfit her mother had helped her to select for the evening. She wore a navy-blue waist cincher and a baby blue blouse with a deep v-neck. While other women – and some of the men – wore pendants or lines of pearls, Nessie had no such accessory. Instead, she bravely showed off the diamond-shaped sheet of brass that had replaced her sternum in a procedure that cured her from a lifetime of chronic illness. In the keyhole at the center of her chest, she had fitted a replica of her wind-up heart's brass turnkey.

She didn't usually show it off like this, tending to wear loose-fitting dresses with high collars, but the Public Gala was a special occasion – and her mother had probably talked her into it via weeks of nagging.

Nessie's mother could be a pain.

Dana slid into her spot on the other side of Jon, trying to inconspicuously transfer his weight from Benedict's shoulder to her arm.

Grateful for her help, he poured the rest of his ale into her matching glass.

Lifting the glass in a mock toast, Dana thanked him back.

"Ah, Mr. Dickenson and the lovely Lady Ailey. It's a pleasure to see you both again." Dr. Addler didn't seem at all enthused. He looked rather bored.

And honestly, Benedict couldn't blame him; the party mostly consisted of drinking and talking. There wasn't even proper music, though he still wouldn't have danced if there had been.

Dr. Addler pivoted to speak to Dr. Blake. "I've heard you've paired off with one of the heirs to Ailey Industries." As if the rest of them weren't there, he waved a lazy finger between Jon and Benedict. "So, which one did you decide on?"

Offering a knowing smile that many mistook for a prideful one, Dana tilted her head and let her long bangs fall over the label of her suit-jacket – she often wore all of her hair in a bun on the back of her head, but Nessie or Nessie's nagging mother must've convinced her to change it up, leave her bangs out of it. "The youngest."

Nodding a little, Dr. Addler turned to Jon and pulled a face seated somewhere between dissent and confusion. "The drunk one." He raised his glass to them as he turned away, speaking with no intonation, "Huzzah to you." He disappeared back into the crowd.

Despite Addler's obvious disgust at the thought, Dana looked smug.

Little did Dr. Addler or anyone else expect that when she said she was courting the youngest heir, she meant Nessie Ailey.

"That was extremely attractive," Nessie whispered across Benedict and Jon. "I could kiss you right now."

With her normal volume, Dana smiled politely to her secret girlfriend. "Lady Ailey have you learned the life-saving technique of mouth-to-mouth?"

Nessie giggled. "I don't believe I have." She turned to Benedict with a small smile. "You'll have to excuse me for a second. The doctor has something educational to show me." With that, Nessie strode toward the supposedly-forbidden hallway.

Dumping Jon back on Benedict, Dana followed.

Jon's eyes followed them, glassy and muddled from his choice and quantity of drink. "One of these days, someone else is going to hop on that bandwagon and ask Dana to teach them mouth-to-mouth, as well."

It was fairly obvious by the longing in his voice that Jon had a crush.

"Is that someone going to be you?" Benedict tried to ignore the sinking feeling in his in his chest.

Grinning wide, Jon turned to him. "You betcha."

www.ingramcontent.com/pod-product-compliance
Lightning Source LLC
Chambersburg PA
CBHW070930130626
46555CB00001B/360